You Only Marry Once

Secrets and Vows Book 1

Gayle Callen

Copyright

Praise for Compromised

"A delightful story with engaging characters. For an enjoyable read, don't miss Compromised."
Romance Reviews Today

"A tempting historical from Gayle Callen."
Romantic Times Magazine

Dedication

To Maggie Shayne, dear friend and writing buddy, who answers my questions, commiserates with my problems, and is always there when I need her.

Chapter 1

London, 1485

"Whom shall I flirt with?" Lady Elizabeth Stanwood murmured to herself, as she stood on tiptoes and searched the large, gilt-ceilinged room, crowded with dancing couples. She was through waiting for the eligible Lord Wyndham to ask for her hand in marriage—she was one and twenty, and it was time to do something to make it happen.

She had tried everything else: saving him the first dance at every ball, catching his eye and giving him a secret smile, showing animated interest whenever he talked about dogs. After all, she liked dogs, too. Didn't he see they might have other things in common? She was heartened that he visited her regularly, brought her little gifts, showed an interest in gaining her father's favor, all actions that indicated an imminent proposal. But it had yet to happen.

So Elizabeth was taking the desperate measure of finding a man to make his lordship jealous. She wasn't certain whom she was looking for; an acquaintance would surely play along with her scheme, but a stranger might make the evening all the more interesting for her and unnerving for Lord Wyndham.

She caught a glimpse of Sir Ralph Cobham and quickly looked away. She had had to repeatedly dissuade him from asking her father for her hand in marriage. There was an underhandedness about the man that made her dislike him, so she certainly couldn't use *him* to make Lord Wyndham jealous.

Then she saw a newcomer step into the room, and her eyes narrowed as she examined him. He was tall, taller than most of the men in attendance, with a breadth of shoulders which needed no padding. His clothing was years out of fashion, only a simple short tunic, belted at the waist, with a cloak thrown back over those impressive shoulders—as if it was not the hottest summer of her memory. His legs were thick and sturdy under his plain hose, and he wore a flat cap over close-cropped brown hair. His strong-jawed face was unshaven, appearing stark amidst the hall's plenitude of curled beards.

Though woefully out of place, he didn't appear ill at ease. Could he be someone's idea of entertainment, a jest to enliven the party? She frowned on such arrogance by the aristocracy, but it had been known to happen.

Whatever he was, the man was perfect for Elizabeth's plan. She gulped the last of her wine, then smiled as she slowly made her way through the crowd, dropping small, perfect curtsies to the noblemen, dipping her head modestly to the ladies, but all the while keeping her gaze on the newcomer.

It wasn't long before he saw her. He glanced away, then his gaze returned to her with satisfying swiftness. She allowed her smile to deepen, to grow mysterious in that way that her suitors had long admired. As his gaze dropped down her body, she took a deep breath, amused when he seemed in a hurry to return to her face. Was he embarrassed to be caught ogling her? How unusual.

No one came up to greet the stranger; he stood alone, at ease, glancing about him with interest. It was as if he were put directly in Elizabeth's path for her purposes.

Compromised

She walked ever nearer, aware of the faintest thrill as his height towered ever higher above her, making her feel delicate and feminine. Surely it was her over-indulgence of wine that was inspiring her imagination.

When she finally stopped before him, the stranger's eyes widened for a moment.

"Good evening, my lord," she murmured, and when he didn't deny the noble title, she relaxed ever so slightly. He was of the aristocracy, guaranteeing that Lord Wyndham would be threatened by his attention to her.

"My lady," he responded.

His deep, gruff voice sent a shiver through her; she had always loved the rich tones of a man's voice.

Once again his appreciative gaze dropped to her amply-revealed bosom, and she surprised herself by blushing, surely due to the warmth in the great hall. When was the last time a man's attention had made her blush? Oh, she'd been an eligible maiden for too long.

She suddenly remembered Lord Wyndham, and turned to see if he had noticed her. But he was deep in conversation with their host, the Marquess of Worcester. Elizabeth frowned.

"Are you waiting for someone, my lady?" the man asked softly.

"Nay." She glanced back up as he leaned toward her. She felt the faintest touch of his breath on her cheek, and it was strangely pleasant. He was close enough now for her to smell the outdoors about him, to feel the heat of his presence. For a moment, she was slightly overwhelmed.

But no, he was only a man, with ordinary brown hair and ordinary brown eyes. Never had a man been born who could resist her charms. It was time to attract Lord Wyndham's notice.

"My lord," she began softly, "the dancing is about to begin. Would you partner with me?"

"Regretfully no, my lady," he said. "I do not dance—at least not this sort of dancing."

"What other kind is there?"

"The country dances of my home," he answered, "but they are performed much…closer together."

His voice had dropped, become almost husky. This time she noticed a faint accent. She thought she should ask him where he came from, but once again his gaze drifted down her body, and she had the uncanny feeling that her skin heated wherever his gaze touched.

"Perhaps someday you can show me these dances," she found herself saying with a sudden breathlessness.

What was wrong with her? He was only a simple man from the country. She mustn't care that his presence loomed large and rugged before her. She had to remind herself of her purpose. She glanced once more at Lord Wyndham, who finally sent her the smallest frown.

Elizabeth smiled up at the stranger. "Would you care to accompany me to the refreshment table? The wine this evening is excellent."

She waited for him to hold his arm out to her, and when he didn't, she wet her lips and bravely slid her arm through his, feeling deliciously warmed by the heat of his body. She was suddenly very glad her parents were not in attendance this evening, and that it had been so easy to distract her youngest brother Nicholas by urging him to flirt with a woman new to court.

Now she felt Lord Wyndham—and others—watching her. She had not done anything truly scandalous, just enough to make her feel an unusual thrill of excitement.

Soon, she and the stranger both held goblets of wine, and they studied each other as they drank.

John Malory was doing his best to conceal his surprise. He'd never been to London, though he'd been told the nobility here lived a different kind of life than he did in the north. He was used to women waiting for his attention, the deference they always felt was due him. Perhaps they'd even felt a sort of fear. He'd grown larger than his parents, larger than his brother, and it bothered him that he intimidated so many. So he'd come to London to make a fresh start at finding a wife.

Oh, he had doubts that this comely woman before him had marriage on her mind. He was just the newest face, the newest amusement. But if this was how London women greeted strangers, he would be going to more parties.

She was not the kind of woman he was seeking, with her rare beauty of which she seemed very aware. Her wheat blonde hair hung in maidenly curls down her back, tumbling over her shoulders past her impressive breasts. Jewels clung to her hair, shimmering with candlelight when she but inclined her head. Her breasts were full and round, and he imagined their heavy weight would fill his hands with pleasure. She obviously wanted them looked at, because she showed much of them so readily.

But it was her secretive green eyes which held him enthralled. There was mischief in her gaze, leaving him feeling pleasantly off-guard. He might enjoy these strange London flirting customs.

He watched her mouth as she sipped the wine, let his glance linger on the curve of her throat as she swallowed. Her skin would be so soft to touch. She was a pretty thing, and he was certain some man would find her perfect as a wife.

But not him.

He gave another regretful glance at her breasts. Ah, he could think of other things he'd like to do with her. Then he chastised himself for such base thoughts.

She leaned closer to smile up at him, and he felt the first heady taste of forbidden passion.

She was dangerous, this one, and he should move on to women more suitable to be his wife. But still he stood at her side, looked his fill, and imagined her warming his bed. He was suddenly glad for the tunic which fell to his thighs and hid how she aroused him.

"How is it that I have never seen you before, my lord?"

"I am new to London, my lady."

"New? In all of your life, you have never been here before?"

She seemed shocked and disbelieving at such a notion, and he hid a smile.

" 'Tis at least five days' journey from my home, my lady. I have not found it necessary to travel to London before now."

He waited for her to ask why, imagined scaring her away by telling of his quest. But again she looked past him at someone else.

He felt a sudden stab of unease—surely it was not jealousy. He hardly expected his simple conversation to hold the attention of a sophisticated woman whose name he didn't even know.

But this evening it seemed important to prove to himself that he hadn't made a mistake by coming to London. He smiled at her, and was rewarded by her full attention again. In fact, she seemed to be looking him over as much as he was looking at her.

He took her free hand in his, and when she stiffened, he rubbed his thumb over her knuckles.

The woman stared at their joined hands, then raised her wide, luminous eyes to his. He felt his breath catch in his throat and heard the most ridiculous words leave his mouth.

"This room has become overly warm, my lady. There is a full moon tonight—perhaps we could look upon it together?" He laid her trembling hand upon his chest over his racing heart.

John kept expecting her to pull away, to alert everyone with her screaming. But she only stared at her hand where it touched him and nodded.

"There is a door to the garden near here," she said in a soft but clear voice. Then she linked her fingers with his to lead him away.

Elizabeth felt excited and warm—and terrified. Could she have consumed too much wine? She had never done anything so wild, and though somewhere in her mind she heard the word, "No!" she was powerless to listen. The need to make Lord Wyndham jealous was fast fading beneath the heated passion in this stranger's eyes.

She pushed open the tall, lead-paned doors leading to the garden and drew the man out with her. Immediately it was like breathing in hot, wet steam. The heat of the day had not dissipated; it clung in wet droplets to the foliage and rose like a mist from the hot ground. The moon illuminated overgrown paths where stone benches peered out as if from secret hideaways.

Elizabeth let go of the stranger's hand, keeping her back to him. Perspiration broke out on her face and chest, and she felt the strangest need to pluck her garments away from her skin.

Suddenly, he rested his hands on her shoulders. She froze, feeling his nearness at her back and the hot heaviness of his large, rough hands, half-afraid and half-excited to find out what he meant to do.

"Would you like to dance?" he asked softly.

"But you said—"

"I could teach you my dancing."

Surely it was his voice weaving this strange languorous spell through her. "You may," she whispered.

"I have your permission, do I?"

Was he laughing at her? She turned around and looked up into his face, shadowed by the night. He wasn't smiling as he slipped an arm around her waist. She gasped as he brought her up against his well-muscled body, then began to turn her about the stone terrace, faster and faster.

The earth tilted away from her as he put his arm beneath her knees and swung her up into the air. With a little cry, she flung her arms around his neck. She was breathing hard, surely from fear, and he was breathing just as heavily.

"Put me down, my lord," she commanded, but it sounded weak even to herself.

He grinned and dropped her legs, letting her slide down the length of his body. And then she felt what a man's codpiece normally kept hidden.

For an astonished moment, Elizabeth hung suspended against him, her toes only brushing the ground, feeling a strange, tense heat blossom low in her belly. She didn't know where to look, what to do, until finally she raised her gaze to his.

Shadows etched his face, his cheekbones high and sharp. His eyes stared at her with a passionate heat that made her forget any other sensation but this. And then she was looking at his mouth.

Suddenly, he lifted her higher and touched his lips to hers. The sweet shock of it sent a shudder through her. She'd never been kissed, had never wanted to allow a man to do such a thing to her before marriage.

But it felt wonderful. His lips were expressive, gentle, so soft as they moved against hers. She kissed him back, barely noticing that he was carrying her deeper into the garden, away from the lights of the house. He sat down on a bench with her in his lap, and she caressed his shoulders, his strong neck.

He threaded his hands through her hair then cupped her face in warmth. He tilted his head, his kisses growing more insistent, his mouth opening against hers. She didn't understand what he wanted until his tongue rasped along her lips. She was startled as an arrow of heat lanced through her, and with a soft moan, she opened her mouth. His tongue invaded, met with hers, and danced until she tentatively responded. The party, her problems, everything retreated except for the moist heat of him. When her tongue finally entered his mouth, he groaned and clutched her tighter to him, pressing her aching breasts to his chest.

Every part of her felt alive and needy and so sensitive to his touch. He moved his hands down her back, rubbing, caressing. He pressed kisses along her cheek, blew softly in her ear until she shivered. She tilted her head back as he nuzzled at her neck and licked along her collar bone. Her fluttering hands touched his shoulders, then flattened along his chest, until he surprised her by shuddering.

When she pulled away, he groaned against her neck. "Nay, please touch me," he whispered.

She gladly gave in to her curiosity and explored his hard, muscular chest as he pressed his mouth ever nearer to her breasts. That inspired a single moment of clarity where she knew she should stop him.

But then he licked between her breasts, and she had to bite her lip to keep from crying out at the pleasure of it. He suddenly lifted her until she was straddling him, and although her skirts were bunched between them, he cupped her buttocks and pulled her hard toward his hips. The pressure there, between her legs, felt like nothing she'd ever imagined—hot and throbbing and so forbidden. For a wild moment, she wished there were no garments between them.

Smoothing his hands down over her shoulders, he slid his fingers beneath her neckline. She held his head to her, her breath coming in panting gasps as she watched what he did to her. With only a twist of his hands, her breasts spilled free.

Neither of them moved for an endless moment. Before she could feel embarrassed, he cupped her breasts in his hands and looked into her face.

"You're beautiful," he whispered hoarsely.

When he rubbed his thumbs across her nipples, she gasped and clung to his shoulders. He watched her face while he caressed her, and she couldn't look away from him. Every movement of his fingers sent a pulse of desire through her, and it all seemed to be centered between her legs.

Then he bent his head and took her breast in his mouth, and the endless possibilities of passion stretched out before her. He moved back and forth between her breasts; every tug of his mouth made the pressure and wanting build up inside her. She didn't know what she wanted, only that he never stop making her feel this alive.

She felt his hands beneath her skirts, sliding up her legs, caressing her skin. How much longer could she bear this wanting, this needing? With a groan, she pressed her hips harder to his. His thumbs formed little circles on the inside of her thighs. She suddenly felt a rush of warm air, and realized he'd pressed her skirts back. She was truly naked to him now, except for her gown bunched at her waist. But the thought only aroused her as she pressed her breasts against his mouth, and let his hands explore her.

And then he touched her in a most private place, where she'd never imagined a man wanting to touch.

And it was paradise.

He frantically kissed her mouth, her breasts, but his fingers moved at such a slow, taunting pace she wanted to urge him faster. She was mindless with the new and overwhelming sensations. So this was why men and women were drawn together; this was why they risked their very reputations to—

"Elizabeth!"

The male voice whispering her name from far away brought her first sense of unease.

"Please, my lord," she began breathlessly, then groaned. She was actually wet down there, and she tried to tighten her thighs in embarrassment. His fingers started circling on her flesh, finding a new, secret place that made every part of her body shake.

But her unease was growing, and she looked around, but saw no one. From farther away, she heard her name called again. She knew she had to stop this before the worst happened, and she was compromised. What could she have hoped to accomplish with this insane plan?

11

"My lord, you must stop!" her voice was louder now, stronger. She caught his hands and pulled them away from her, while scooting back toward his knees. Her body was bereft, aching with the need for something now out of reach, something only he knew how to give her, and she quickly got to her feet, her skirts spilling down around her. Between her thighs, she felt swollen, aching.

He tilted his head back, and in the moonlight he looked severe with pain. Did he feel it too, even though she hadn't touched him as he'd done to her?

"You're right," he murmured hoarsely.

His voice was enough to make her want to collapse against him in surrender.

"We shouldn't have come out here," he continued. "I shouldn't have—"

He broke off as he looked at her again. Elizabeth realized her breasts were still bared, white in the moonlight, and she quickly tucked them back into her bodice, suffused by a hot feeling of shame. She desperately wished she could pull the neckline higher, but her attempts only made him wince.

"Tell me your name," he whispered. "Let me come to visit you."

"Oh, no, you mustn't! There's a man—"

"You're married!" he said, too loudly.

"Shh!" She looked back over her shoulder, and her panic only increased at how foolish it was to be out here alone with a man. And now she knew the reason why. She would be lucky if it was only her brother who found them. "Nay, I'm not married, but I never should have done this. There's a man inside who wants to marry me."

He surged to his feet to tower over her. "He is in there now? You deliberately brought me out here, hoping he was watching us?"

"Nay, I—I forgot about him," she insisted, beginning to back away from this stranger who fascinated her, yet frightened her. What could she have been thinking? She knew nothing about him. And though she'd originally wanted Lord Wyndham to notice her, this was not what she had wanted him to see.

"You used me to make him jealous, when he damn well could have come out here and found us together!"

"I—I never thought—"

"That is very obvious, my lady. You don't think much, do you?"

She stiffened in anger. "There is no need for insults! It was your idea to be alone with me."

"And your quick suggestion where we could go. You even took my hand and led me, by God, so don't play the innocent with me." He advanced on her. "Do you do this every evening, pick the most gullible man and taunt him with your beauty, then deny him that which you promised?"

"I promised nothing!" she cried, shaking with her fury—and her rising fright. "I never meant any of this to happen, and I certainly have never done such a thing before!"

"Maybe you'd be married by now, if you'd chosen to arouse that other man you're so anxious to please."

They glared at each other, both breathing hard.

"Elizabeth!"

She winced, hearing Nicholas's voice a moment before she saw him. Her brother, just coming into manhood and thinner than the stranger, swept past a tree and into view, then halted with his mouth dropping open.

"Elizabeth?" His spoke her name in confusion and growing worry.

The stranger looked over his shoulder at Nicholas, his body stiff.

"My brother," she murmured. "I have to go. I'm sorry that I—that this—"

The tall, imposing stranger caught her arm when she tried to go past him, and spoke in a low voice. "You're not sorry. I'm only surprised you didn't wait for your own pleasure before you denied me mine."

She shook her head, confused by what he meant.

"Unhand her!" said Nicholas, striding toward them, his hand on the hilt of his sword.

Oh God, what had she done? She put up a placating hand toward her brother. " 'Tis fine, we were simply speaking. I'll come with you."

But Nicholas was grimly looking up at the much taller man, who let her arm go. "What do you think you are doing with my sister?"

"Nothing!" Elizabeth insisted before the stranger could speak.

Nicholas looked the man up and down. "I know not where you're from, sir, but here you do not force a woman to be alone with you!"

The stranger arched a dark brow at her, and Elizabeth felt herself blush. There'd been no forcing involved, and they both knew it.

"Nicholas, please, do not make a scene. This kind man will tell no one about our discussion, *will you*?" She gave the stranger a pointed look.

For a moment, he said nothing, and her heart skipped a beat. She didn't know him, knew nothing about him. He could be a scoundrel. What if this had been some sort of plan, and she'd fallen into his trap?

The stranger bowed from the waist before saying, "I apologize for my thoughtlessness. I will say nothing."

Her brittle smile was full of relief. "There, Nicholas, cease your insults and escort me back inside. Help me make up for my silly mistake. We were just talking, I promise."

She yanked her brother's arm hard and he reluctantly allowed her to pull him back toward the terrace. But he stopped when they reached the tall glass doors. There was no one else on the terrace, and she tried to take her first relaxed breath. It wasn't easy.

Nicholas put his hands on her shoulders and looked directly into her eyes. "Elizabeth, this foolishness has to stop."

"Foolishness?" she echoed, widening her eyes with innocence.

"You cannot make Lord Wyndham ask for your hand in such a ridiculous and risky way."

"I was not trying to make—"

"Then what were you trying to do?"

She bit her lip, then reluctantly admitted, "Trying to get him to notice me. I wanted to flirt, to show him that many men found me attractive, and that he shouldn't wait too long."

Nicholas groaned and briefly closed his eyes. "You have more sense than this, regardless of what our parents keep telling you."

She winced at the memories of her parents telling her over and over that it was fortunate that she was beautiful and wealthy because she had nothing else to offer a man.

"They're wrong," Nicholas said softly. "You're clever."

She gave him a bitter smile. "Really? Would you still say that after tonight?"

She slipped into the open doors to the great hall and disappeared into the anonymity of the crowd.

Chapter 2

Elizabeth awoke late the next morning and stared blindly up at the canopy over her four-poster bed, feeling damp and overly warm from the oppressing heat. She had had a difficult time falling asleep, and even then slept fitfully, with dreams of the stranger haunting her, kissing her, caressing her, making her feel somehow unfulfilled.

She rolled over and covered her head with the pillow. How could she have been so foolish? She knew her father believed her less than intelligent, and now she'd proven it. She thought of the words she'd once overheard between her parents, how they'd told each other to emphasize Elizabeth's beauty, because it was all she had besides a dowry to entice a man.

Well, it had worked, she thought bitterly. The stranger had certainly not been enticed by her clever conversation. She felt the tears start again, but she conquered them before they could fall. She would not cry over her stupidity. Her mistake was finished, and luckily no one had seen them out...groping in the garden.

When her maid came to help her dress, the girl seemed particularly wary, and wouldn't meet Elizabeth's eyes.

Elizabeth finally touched her arm. "Matilda, is something wrong?"

The girl shook her head, her little linen cap dipping to cover her eyes. Then suddenly she twisted her hands

17

together, took a deep breath and looked Elizabeth in the face.

"Milady, yer father just seems…upset. He had a visitor early this morn, and now the man is back. I brought them ale, and they barely stopped their arguin' 'til I was gone."

Elizabeth felt a cold shiver of dread. "Is the stranger a…tall, broad man, dressed plainly?" Even now she could remember the width of his shoulders beneath her exploring hands, and she cursed her good memory—not an asset her parents could brag about.

"Nay, milady, he's rather…short, on the puny side, even."

Elizabeth gripped the back of a chair and tried not to sway with relief. She was so worried that the stranger would find her and tell her parents what a sinful woman she was. My God, he could even try to blackmail her into further intimacies. How much more proof was necessary before she realized she truly was a foolish woman?

With Matilda's help, Elizabeth dressed in a sedate blue gown with a square neckline above which her delicate chemise reached to her throat. It was difficult to feel decently covered. She could still vividly remember the stranger's hands on her breasts, his fingers stroking between her thighs.

Her face flushed, Elizabeth said, "Thank you, Matilda. I'll be down to break my fast shortly."

Just as the maid opened the door, they heard the earl's loud voice. "Elizabeth! Come down here at once."

She blanched as she realized how her father's voice carried up the marble staircase from the front hall. He had never before shouted at her like that. Her heavy gown clung to her damp skin and choked her neck. When her knees almost buckled, she held the door frame for support, nodding into Matilda's terrified face.

"You go on about your day, Matilda. 'Tis me he wants to see."

The girl bobbed a curtsy and fled toward the back staircase. Elizabeth gazed after her wistfully, wishing she too could escape. Even though the stranger had not come for her, she had a horrible, sinking feeling of dread.

When she stepped into her father's withdrawing room, she was startled to see Sir Ralph Cobham sitting in the seat of honor before the hearth. The look he shot her was malevolent, triumphant—had he convinced her father to accept a marriage proposal?

She warily faced the Earl of Chelmsford, only to find his dignified face cold and remote, as if she were a stranger.

"Father, you wanted to see me?" Her voice sounded high-pitched, not like her own.

He didn't invite her to sit down, so she stood with her hands fisted in her skirts, as if waiting for her executioner.

"Earlier this morn, Sir Ralph told me a tale that I could not easily dismiss."

For a moment, she felt confused. This wasn't a marriage proposal?

"What went on at the party last night, the one your mother and I couldn't attend?" Every word grew colder and colder, as if icicles should be dangling from his lips.

She dug her fingernails into her palms, and her stomach quivered with nausea. "I danced, I talked to people, I—"

"Did you go into the garden with a strange man?"

"I—" She shot a wild glance at Sir Ralph, who sat back and folded his arms over his narrow chest, as if waiting for an enjoyable play to commence.

"Did you go into the garden with a strange man!"

Her father barked out the words so furiously that Elizabeth stumbled back a step from his disgust.

"We just walked!" she cried, and the first embarrassing tear slipped down her cheek. The lie almost choked her, but she had no choice. Had Sir Ralph followed them— stood in the shadows and watched? She felt like retching.

"Sir Ralph," her father said, in a calmer voice, "what did you see?"

Some of Sir Ralph's triumph faded. "I was dancing with Mistress Penelope, my lord. I only know that your daughter was gone a long time, and when she returned—alone—her face was flushed and her clothing disheveled."

Before her father could speak, she demanded, "How was my clothing 'disheveled'? The wind had—"

"There was no wind, Elizabeth," her father said in a low voice.

"Father, do you believe the things he is implying? He holds a grudge against me because I do not return his affections. He would enjoy seeing me humiliated!"

"It is easy to know the truth," her father answered. "I have sent for the man in question."

"How did you find him? He had only just arrived in London." Elizabeth tried to tell herself this was a good thing, that all the stranger had to do was repeat her denial, and there would be no proof.

"Sir Ralph told me that he is a distant cousin to your host. I sent my men to learn what they could of him." He paused, and eyed her almost contemptuously. "Do you even know his name?"

She felt her face flame with embarrassment. "No," she finally said, lifting her chin.

"John Malory." He sat down at his desk and they all remained silent, waiting.

John Malory, she thought to herself, sitting as far away from Sir Ralph as she could. John. A plain name for a plainly dressed man, a man who now held her fate in his hands. And she'd given him that power over her.

~oOo~

John was shown into the palatial home of the Earl of Chelmsford, and he followed the maid through an immense hall, lined with marble columns, with floor tiles laid out like vines.

He shook his head to clear it. He had no idea why he'd been sent for, what an earl could possibly want of him. John had told his cousin, the Marquess of Worcester, that he didn't need help. Recalling his cousin's worried look, John now wondered if that had been a mistake.

The maid showed him into a withdrawing room, which had tall rows of windows along two walls. He almost had to squint at the two men who'd risen as he entered. But as his sight adjusted, he could see that they were strangers to him.

There was another movement on his right, and he saw that it was the woman from the garden. In his mind he was suddenly in the dark, hot garden again, with her in his lap. He could see the woman's green eyes turn sultry, just at the moment he'd bared her breasts. The frustration of their encounter hadn't left him, and now he was facing her again.

21

By daylight she still wore her beauty with an immense dignity, even though her face looked strained and pale as she stared at him.

"John Malory?" said one of the men.

John turned to the older man, who could only be the nobleman who'd summoned him. He wore power like his daughter wore beauty.

"Aye, my lord?" he asked, feeling a knot of tension tighten in his stomach.

"I am the Earl of Chelmsford, and this is Sir Ralph Cobham. In worry for my daughter's reputation—"

John thought he heard a strangled sound from the woman behind him.

"—Sir Ralph wished me to know that you and my daughter Elizabeth were seen leaving the party together last night. Can you defend your actions?"

For a moment, John was stunned, then full of anger at his own stupidity. Shouldn't he have known that liberties taken with a noblewoman would return to haunt him? Then he remembered her willingness, and wondered if she had deliberately set out to make a fool of him. By the looks of her father's mansion, the woman did not need to marry for wealth, so what was going on?

John looked at Cobham, saw the cold pleasure he was obviously taking from the woman's humiliation, and knew the kind of man he was. He would spread tales across London, maybe all of England, to appease this obvious hatred he had for her—for Elizabeth. The woman who'd been living in his dreams now had a name.

John turned to look at her again, and if anything, her face had grown paler. Had she led Cobham on, too, only to throw his desire back in his face?

Compromised

John clenched his hands behind his back. His dreams of having a wife like his brother's faded into the ashes of his own foolishness. He could not let the girl suffer alone for what they both had done.

"I went into the garden with your daughter, my lord, that is true."

"And?"

My God, what did the man want from him, details? "We kissed," he said shortly.

The earl slammed his hand down on the desk in anger, Cobham practically burst with the pleasure of his revenge, and Elizabeth gave a startled cry.

"That's not true!" she said.

He suddenly realized that she had lied to her father to protect herself. Didn't the foolish woman know it was too late, that even if they both denied it, the rumors would ruin her?

"He must want my dowry, Father, surely you see that!"

John flinched at the insult, and turned his cold gaze on her. "I did not seek this meeting out, my lady. Nor did I force you into the garden."

Now it was her turn to draw back as if he'd slapped her.

"You and my daughter will be married," the earl said shortly. "We will have a special license procured quickly."

John felt a flush creep up his neck as he saw how disappointed the man obviously was at the thought of his daughter marrying so low.

Elizabeth approached her father, who stepped away. For a brief moment, John felt sympathy for her.

"But Father, we know nothing about him! He could be a—a tradesman for all we know!"

John's sympathy evaporated.

"He is a baron," the earl said, "and for that, you should be thankful. Sir Ralph, you may leave us now."

Cobham looked disappointed as he got to his feet. When the earl said nothing else, John made it a point to block the doorway and tower over the wretch.

"Lady Elizabeth is going to be my wife," he said in a low, cold voice. "Should I hear even one unsavory rumor, I will know who started it." He leaned close to Cobham's pale, twitching face. "And I will hunt you down."

Cobham darted around him and fled the room. In the heavy silence, John saw Elizabeth staring wide-eyed at him.

"I didn't do that just for you," he said shortly, "but also for the honor of my family."

She flinched, and he suddenly wished he could take back the hurtful words. Their situation was not her fault alone.

In a quieter, calmer voice, John said, "Leave us now, Lady Elizabeth. Your father and I have much to discuss—and you have to pack."

"Pack?" she whispered in a weak voice. "Where are we going?"

"Yorkshire, my home."

That seemed to shock her more than their marriage. He caught a glimpse of her glistening eyes before she lowered her head and hurried from the room.

~oOo~

Elizabeth shook with suppressed tears, but she could not cower in her bedchamber. She sat on the stairs in the hall, watching the door behind which her father and that man—John Malory—planned her life without even considering her.

24

Compromised

Lord Malory had ordered her from the room, and her father had allowed it! What could they be saying?

The front door opened, and Nicholas entered the cool shadows of the front hall. He saw her almost immediately, frowning. "Elizabeth, what are you doing perched on the stairs?"

She opened her mouth, but her throat felt choked with suppressed grief.

He took the stairs two at a time and then sat beside her. "What is it, sister, dear?"

"The man from the garden…he's in the withdrawing room with Father. They're planning our wedding even as we speak."

Nicholas took a swift breath, then cursed. "So he's taking advantage of you."

"No, yes—I don't know. Sir Ralph told Father he saw us in the garden. Father sent for Lord Malory—"

"That's the stranger's name?"

"He—he's a baron from the north. The *far* north." She shivered. "*Yorkshire*! Oh, God, Nicholas, what if they truly ship me to *Yorkshire* with an impoverished baron!"

"Wait, slow down. What happened?"

She explained about Sir Ralph's revenge, John Malory's confession, and the current discussion of her wedding.

Nicholas gripped her hand. "Oh, Elizabeth, I'm sorry. I should never have left your side. You would never have gone off with a stranger if I'd been there."

"Don't blame yourself," she whispered, filled with regret. "I made certain you were distracted."

He grimaced. "But marriage to a stranger—we can talk Father out of that. What if I challenge the man?"

"No!" she said harshly. "You will not pay for my stupidity. I would never be able to live with myself. I—I've never seen Father like this. He is furious with me, maybe even…*done* with me."

Nicholas gripped her hand harder and said nothing for a moment. His presence usually made her happy, gave her a sense of peace. But now she didn't know if she'd ever have that again—perhaps she'd never even *see* her brothers again. She'd once had a friend marry a man from Lancashire and never return to London again. Her letters had become infrequent and then absent altogether.

"My life is over," Elizabeth whispered.

"Do not say such things! Lord Malory could have abandoned you to ruination, after all."

"Abandoned my money? Hardly."

"Elizabeth, a dowry comes with every highborn marriage. You know that."

She gritted her teeth and didn't answer. She knew it was true, but had always thought her dowry a gift offered to her husband—not that he'd really *need* it.

"If they make you go," Nicholas said, "I will accompany you."

She gave him a faint smile, studying his dear face as if it were one of the last times she ever would. "That is a sweet offer, but no, I won't take you from London, from your studies, from your future. And Father won't allow it, I can already tell." She shivered at the contempt she'd seen on the earl's face.

She had gotten herself into this mess, all because she'd tried to make Lord Wyndham jealous. And now he'd never ask to marry her. The wonderful life she'd expected for herself was gone.

26

Compromised

When the door opened, she rose quickly to her feet. Lord Malory emerged alone and closed the door behind him. He walked across the hall, unaware of her presence, his face pensive and distracted. Where was his triumph? Surely he only concealed it well.

Nicholas gripped her hand even tighter, and she gave him a warning frown. She could not allow her sweet brother to embroil himself in her mess.

Lord Malory saw them and stopped. She had forgotten how imposing he was, how even in his plain garments he seemed large in her father's overpowering hall.

"Did you wish to speak with me, Lady Elizabeth?"

"I have nothing to say to you," she said in a low voice, hating the quiver he would certainly hear. She had death grip on Nicholas's hand, whether to support herself or keep him in check, she didn't know.

Lord Malory only inclined his head, as if she wasn't even worth arguing with. Her eyes burned with unshed tears. He walked past them and out the door.

She quickly dabbed beneath her wet lashes.

"I should have said—something," Nicholas insisted.

"No, this is not your fight. It's mine and I shall deal with it." With a trembling smile for her brother, she marched to her father's door and knocked.

There was a long silence before he told her to come in. He was sitting at his desk, but staring out the windows to their sprawling garden that sloped down to the Thames. He didn't look at her; he didn't speak.

Every feeling of unworthiness she'd ever had crowded into her head. When her mother returned from the country, Elizabeth would have to explain it all again. And her mother might ask exactly what she had done in that garden.

She was every bit the stupid girl they thought she was.

"Father?"

To her horror, her voice broke, and the tears finally spilled down her cheeks. She wanted her father to hold her, to tell her everything would be all right. But he'd never been that kind of man, and he certainly wouldn't start now.

He cleared his throat, but still didn't look at her. "I'll have the license sometime tomorrow. The marriage will take place the next day."

"But Father, surely there is something else we can do. All he wants is my money!"

"Then why did he tell me to keep it for one year, until he'd proven himself?"

She didn't know what to say to that. Finally, she asked, "What about the marriage contract?"

Her father picked up a quill and bent over his desk. "At least he's willing to marry you. Perhaps you should have thought of money before you brazenly kissed him. Now please leave, so I can decide how to tell your mother of your disgrace."

"I—I should be there," she said in a warbling voice.

He eyed her with faint surprise. "I'll send for you when she arrives."

Elizabeth held back her sobs until she was alone in her own room. My God, not only was she to marry a man who expected her to live far from London, but he was impoverished, too. As if marrying her was supposed to make up for that! How could her father allow this to happen?

Compromised

How had *she* allowed this to happen? she wondered dully.

Chapter 3

Elizabeth was called back to the withdrawing room as darkness shadowed the house that evening. She'd dreaded her mother's return all day, sick at the thought of explaining what she'd done and seeing her mother's terrible disappointment.

She arrived before her mother did, although she heard the woman calling something to the servants from another room. Her father gazed at her coldly and said nothing, while Elizabeth twisted her hands together and hoped she wouldn't lose her last meal. Not that she'd been able to eat much.

Lady Chelmsford breezed through the open door and smiled in surprise at Elizabeth. Then she caught sight of her glowering husband, and that smile faded into uncertainty.

"Whatever is wrong?" Lady Chelmsford demanded. "Has someone died?" She put a hand to her throat. "Nicholas?"

" 'Tis not your youngest son," the earl said gruffly, "only your daughter's foolishness, which has disgraced us all."

Elizabeth took a shaky breath, feeling his words bruise as much as a physical assault. He hadn't even tried to break the news gently.

"She will be married in two days' time to a baron from Yorkshire, John Malory."

Compromised

Lady Chelmsford's lips opened and closed several times until at last she gave Elizabeth a dazed look. "But…you said we would plan her wedding together. You agreed that Lord Wyndham would be perfect…that I could host the wedding of the year."

Each word was a blow that Elizabeth flinched from. They'd talked wedding clothes and setting up a household since she'd been old enough to understand. She was the only daughter, and her mother had been giddy over the parties and ceremonies and planning to come. And now it was all gone.

"Blame your daughter," the earl said. "She let herself be compromised by a stranger last night, and the damage cannot be undone."

Lady Chelmsford put a hand to her throat and said faintly, "Compromised?"

"We but kissed," Elizabeth said at last. She thought she'd cried out all her tears, but more slid down her cheeks. "I never meant for this to—"

"You never thought it through," her father interrupted harshly. "You never do, and you're making your mother suffer for it."

Aren't I suffering? she thought wildly. *Aren't I the one marrying a stranger?*

When her mother started to cry, Elizabeth felt like she'd been stabbed.

"Go upstairs," her father told her. "I will comfort your mother."

Elizabeth ran all the way there, and was still sobbing an hour later, her lungs aching, her stomach nauseated. Her mother knocked on the door, then entered, having changed into a black gown of mourning. Elizabeth blew her nose for the tenth time. She wanted a hug; she wanted reassurance that everything would be all right, but Lady Chelmsford looked as if the world had ended, making Elizabeth know it truly had.

"Did you…change Father's mind?" Elizabeth whispered.

"That will never happen," her mother said dully, sitting down on a chair near the bed.

Elizabeth had known that truth, but her shoulders sagged regardless. "I have to…go?"

"To Yorkshire, aye."

"Mama, it is so far away." Now she truly sounded like a little girl, and she silently berated herself. "Will you visit me?"

"I know not. It is up to your father." Lady Chelmsford sighed. "The court has lost a great beauty, and the other heiresses will be glad of it."

"Oh, not Katherine!" Her dearest friend, Lady Katherine Berkeley, would never wish her gone.

"All of those who wanted Lord Wyndham for themselves now have a clear path to him." She shook her head. "You foolish girl."

"I'm sorry, Mama," Elizabeth whispered.

"We had such plans for you. And now you have shamed us."

She could barely breathe around the sob lodged in her throat.

"But do not fear the worst," Lady Chelmsford continued. "Your father is letting it be known that yours is a desperate love match, that Lord Malory cannot wait to claim you as his own."

Compromised

Elizabeth drew her knees up to her chest and hugged them. *A love match?* she thought bitterly. "So...Lord Malory and I will have to pretend before all of London..."

"No, the wedding will be a private affair. I once thought London would see you resplendent and happy and in love. But that's gone now." She sighed. "Will people believe this great love match? Considering Lord Malory only recently arrived, I doubt it, but your father thinks it's for the best."

They sat in awkward, heavy silence. Elizabeth tried to think of a way to make her apology mean more, but her thoughts were scattered and full of panic.

"There is something you should know about the wedding night," her mother said in a formal voice.

Was *this* the talk all her friends had giggled about? Elizabeth had once looked forward to discovering the answer, but now it seemed so very real and alarming.

Lady Chelmsford did not look at her as a slow flush worked its way up to her cheeks. "A man has needs that a wife must fulfill in bed. It will be your duty to do as he wishes, as...often as he wishes. Just close your eyes and bear it until it is finished. The only blessing is that a child might result, if you're lucky."

The only blessing...? But hadn't Lord Malory's caresses been part of what a man and woman shared? Elizabeth wasn't certain that bearing it would be a problem.

"It will hurt the first time," her mother continued.

Elizabeth's eyes widened. "What will hurt?"

"When he is on top of you," Lady Chelmsford said impatiently, then rose to her feet. "It is up to your husband to explain more."

Elizabeth didn't want to approach her wedding night so ignorant. But how could she ask for more details, for her mother's help, when she'd shamed the family already?

~oOo~

But there was one person Elizabeth could confide her fears in, and that was her dearest friend Lady Katherine Berkeley, who'd recently returned from one of her father's castles in the midlands. Katherine had seemed far more subdued and nervous since her arrival in London, but she hadn't wanted to discuss what was bothering her. Elizabeth had meant to pry it out of her, but now, her own problems overwhelmed her. She escaped the house first thing in the morning and was relieved to find her friend at home.

Katherine, blond and delicate, with a sweet nature, took one look at Elizabeth's face, pulled her up to her bedchamber, and shut the door.

Elizabeth hadn't meant to cry, but she found herself sobbing in Katherine's arms. Only when she was hiccuping through the last sob did Katherine withdraw and stare solemnly into her face.

"What is wrong, dearest Elizabeth? It must be terrible."

"I—I am to marry tomorrow."

Katherine's mouth dropped open for a moment before she collected herself.

And then Elizabeth remembered that Katherine had been engaged for years, and her groom had not even visited her during all that time, let alone set a wedding date. "Oh, Katherine, I forgot your situation."

"No, do not think of me. Come, tell me the details."

She drew Elizabeth onto a cushioned window seat where they'd once huddled playing with their dolls. They were carefree girls no longer, Elizabeth thought bitterly. In a flow of words she couldn't control, she told her friend everything that had happened.

Katherine's sympathetic gaze was a comfort. "My dear, I am so sorry."

"Sorry for my stupidity?" Elizabeth laughed without amusement.

"You are not stupid," Katherine said firmly. "I hate how your parents have made you think that. 'Tis obvious you share a connection with this man that was overwhelming once you were alone. You seemed to have liked what he did in the garden," she teased.

"And that's what I don't understand. My mother never said much before about what went on between men and women. And last night she made it sound so…unpleasant."

Katherine bit her lip and looked away.

Elizabeth leaned toward her. "You know something!"

"Not much, and none of it good, I'm afraid."

"So your mother proved just as useless as mine?"

"So far, yes, but I don't know what she'll say on the eve of my wedding."

"Tell me what you know! I don't even *know* this man. How can I let him…" She trailed off. She'd already let him take terrible liberties with her. Her emotions had been overwrought, her thoughts chaotic, her feelings full of wonder and need. But all of that seemed unimportant now that she'd be forced to spend the rest of her life with him, far from London and her friends and family.

"I think you should trust your instincts," Katherine said.

"My instinct is to run screaming as far away as I can!"

"And you know you can't do that. Your first instinct was to trust him enough to be alone with him."

"Well, yes, but…what does that matter? He tried to *seduce* me, Katherine! Haven't we always been told that's what bad men want to do when they get us alone? And I let it happen anyway. And now I am to be punished."

"Try not to think of it that way."

"Listen to you and your optimism," Elizabeth said ruefully. "Lord Bolton has not been a decent betrothed to you."

"I have been unlucky, 'tis true," Katherine murmured. "It could have been worse. I never told you this, but a—a man once tried to force himself on me."

Elizabeth gasped and touched her friend's arm. "When did this happen?"

"Several years ago. The details are irrelevant. I succeeded in escaping with my virtue intact, but the important thing I want you to know is that my mother didn't believe me."

"Oh, Katherine," she whispered.

"At least your parents are trying to do right by you, and so is Lord Malory. I have not given up on the hope of love, and you shouldn't either."

"But how can I love a man who schemed to get my dowry? Why else would he have allowed me to be compromised? My father says he'll tell everyone it's a love match, that we simply couldn't wait to be together. Who will believe that?"

"Every man expects a dowry—you know that."

"But I expected it to be a *gift* he truly didn't need. I was naïve, I guess."

"Try not to fear the worst. It might be better than you imagine."

Compromised

"You'll come to the wedding, won't you? Father is keeping most people away, but I told him that I need you as my witness."

Katherine clasped her hands together. "I'll gladly be there to support you. And I will write and try to visit you. I'm very curious to meet this man you couldn't resist."

Elizabeth sighed.

~oOo~

John was in the stables behind the inn where he'd been staying, looking over the new horses he'd purchased, when he heard someone call his name. He turned around to see Elizabeth's brother glowering at him. And then the man's fist connected with his chin, and John reeled back. His instinct was to defend himself, but instead, he straightened and met the young man's angry gaze.

"We have not yet been introduced," John said dryly.

"Nicholas Stanwood," the young man said. "And you're John Malory, the man who ruined my sister's reputation. You'd better not have ruined her future as well."

"I shall try not to. What else would you like from me besides a pound of flesh?"

"I believe you've done enough, don't you?"

John let out a long breath. "And what would you have had me do differently, refuse to marry your sister?"

With his hands on his hips, Nicholas practically puffed out his chest. "If you'd have behaved as a gentleman, none of this would have happened."

"And you are correct," John said soberly. "I deeply regret it."

"Are you saying my sister isn't worth marrying?" Nicholas countered like a bantam rooster.

"Of course not. I regret that I have disrupted both our lives. Neither of us wanted this, but I intend to do the best of my abilities to be a good husband to your sister."

Nicholas eyed him intently, and then some of the stiffness left his shoulders. He glanced at the horses. "You've made a good choice with the horseflesh."

"Thank you." John hid his amusement at the change of subject. Suddenly, he realized he had an opportunity. "I am serious about being a good husband. Elizabeth seems quite miserable to be leaving London with me. Can you tell me what I should know about her, what would make her happy?"

"You know what would make her happy," Nicholas said dryly, "that this situation would all go away. But other than that…I know Elizabeth is an impulsive woman. Perhaps you both share that trait," he added.

John eyed the younger man with more respect. "That is a good point."

"Be patient with her. She is very loyal once she sets her mind to accepting a person."

"It might take some time for her to accept me."

"It might," Nicholas conceded. "She can be stubborn, but much of that is because of the way we were raised. I don't believe our parents did Elizabeth any favors by commenting endlessly on her beauty."

"It would be difficult not to. Your sister's face is exquisite." He wasn't so certain about what was behind that face, but he could hardly tell her brother that. Her figure was exquisite as well, but he most definitely wouldn't say that to her brother either.

Compromised

"She underestimates her own strengths." Nicholas shook his head. "But I love her, and she is a good, kind person."

I hope so, was all John could think.

Nicholas left as abruptly as he'd arrived. John leaned against the horse stall and rubbed the animal's head in contemplation. Besides his mother, the only woman he was close to was his sister by marriage, Martha. She and his brother William had both been seventeen when they'd married, and they'd had five children in ten years. John had never seen two people more in love, and he told William often that the strength and durability of their marriage was because of Martha. She was gracious and loving, kind to everyone from yeoman to nobleman. Her sweet nature shown from her eyes; John couldn't even have said if she had the sort of beauty admired at court. She had the beauty that truly counted, on the inside. She forgave easily, even when John and William were detained for days later than they'd promised to return home, or when the children ruined her sewing. She made the best of every situation. If John was marrying a woman like Martha, he would be content.

But Elizabeth wasn't Martha. He didn't know what kind of woman she was. He prayed for the patience Nicholas said he would need.

~oOo~

Standing on the steps of the church the next morning, John watched Elizabeth dismount from the pillion seat behind her father's saddle. Pale and red-eyed, she looked wildly around, but not at him.

She clutched her father's arm. "Katherine isn't here!"

39

The earl shook her off. "She probably did not want to be seen at this farce."

John stiffened at the old man's harsh tone.

Elizabeth turned desperate eyes on her mother. "She would never abandon me today. I just saw her yesterday. Where could she be?"

John frowned, but the only person who met his gaze was Nicholas, who strode up the steps to him.

"What is going on?" John demanded.

"Elizabeth said her friend Katherine Berkeley was to be her maid today. She never arrived at our home, and when we sent a servant, her family turned him away. Elizabeth was hoping she'd be here."

"Could she be ill, or called out of London to tend an ill family member?"

Grimly, Nicholas said, "Then why wouldn't the family say that?"

Elizabeth had been close enough to overhear the last part of their conversation, and she stared at John, distraught, as if her last hope for solace had died.

He took her arm. "Should we postpone the wedding for you to see to your friend?"

Her eyes gleamed with tears of hope.

"We will not wait on a foolish girl," Lord Chelmsford thundered, striding past them and up the church stairs.

"But Father—" Elizabeth began.

Nicholas caught her arm. "You know he won't change his mind. I'll find out what happened to Katherine and let you know."

Elizabeth lifted her chin and glared at John, who knew she wanted to blame all her problems on him. And it only got worse.

Compromised

Fighting tears, she trembled through the whole ceremony. It was nothing like his brother William's wedding ceremony, where the bride had been glowing with love, and William's eyes had shone with happy tears. Friends and family had come from far and wide to celebrate with them, and the laughter and music had gone on into the night.

But not John's wedding. There would be no happy memories of this day. He didn't like feeling sympathy for Elizabeth, who had equal share bringing about this disaster. Every young girl expected to have a wonderful wedding some day, and hers was attended by few people. Two of her three brothers were away, and her parents stared at the ground, rather than at her. Nicholas spent the entire ceremony glaring at everyone, including John, when he wasn't given his sister encouraging smiles.

John had been introduced to Lady Chelmsford earlier that morning, and the woman had looked him up and down and promptly burst into tears. It seemed that Elizabeth had not only disgraced herself by becoming entangled with John, but her entire family.

John was having an increasingly difficult time understanding this. He was marrying her, after all.

He had wanted a strong woman who would work at his side, and be able to oversee his castle when he had to travel to his other holdings. But he couldn't imagine Lady Elizabeth Stanwood having those capabilities. He thought of his brother William's wife, Martha, and how capable she was. Everyone admired her, and came to her with their problems and illnesses. She made time for her five children, as well as her husband, if William's satisfied smile was any indication.

A feeling of grief hung heavy about John's heart. He had allowed himself to be swayed by a pretty face and comely body, and he'd have to pay the price.

At the end of the ceremony, Elizabeth pointedly presented her cheek to be kissed, and he knew with grim certainty that it would be an awkward wedding night.

~oOo~

Elizabeth spent her wedding day in a daze. She barely remembered the ceremony, so confused and heartsick were her thoughts, both about her own future and Katherine's mysterious disappearance. The wedding feast was small and tense, and as she sat beside her new husband, she could only think how…plainly-dressed he was, which reminded her that he was poor.

She shuddered and looked about the immense dining chamber of her parents' home. Would she ever see any of this again? Would his entire home fit in this room?

Whenever she felt like crying, she looked at her mother, who was doing all her crying for her. That was all her mother had done since their talk, making Elizabeth feel miserable and guilty.

She had only her maids to lead her up to her bedchamber, since none of her friends had been allowed to attend the wedding. Except for Katherine, who the earl kept insisting surely had something more important to do. But Elizabeth knew that wasn't true. She wanted to send another note to the family, but her father tore it up. She knew he was taking out his anger on anything he could, that he was focused on his own disappointments, but

Compromised

Elizabeth knew something far worse must have happened to Katherine.

As her maids dressed her in a sheer night rail and turned down the bed, Elizabeth clutched her stomach and thought she'd be sick. She knew she was expected to lie with her husband, but the passion of their evening in the garden had fled. At least her anger was returning, she thought, watching as the maids scampered from the chamber and left her alone.

Anger was all she had left to feel, so she fed the flame by remembering Lord Malory's betrayal to her father. Why hadn't he lied and said nothing had happened between them? The only reason could be money, no matter how her father thought otherwise.

And there was no point asking where they'd be living— or even how—because it would only make her more miserable. By not knowing, at least she could still hope.

Chapter 4

John stood outside the bedchamber and told himself to go inside. He was holding a pouch with the wedding gift he'd brought from home, and he wondered if his new wife would throw it back at him.

With a heavy sigh, he gave a brisk knock and opened the door. Elizabeth stood at the window looking out at the last pink of sunset, but she whirled and faced him, her arms folded tightly across her chest. It only took him a moment to realize why. The night rail she wore was made of the sheerest silk and lace; it clung to her hips and outlined even the indentation between her thighs. He stood there stupidly, knowing he was gaping at her, yet unable to stop himself.

"They made me wear this," she said.

He heard the mutiny and anger in her voice, and it broke the spell of desire she so easily wove around him.

"Then I'll help you take the garment off if you'd like," he said mildly. For just a moment, he'd somehow let himself believe she might welcome him.

Instead she glared at him. "Oh, yes, you've already proven how skillful you are at disrobing a woman. You must have had plenty of practice."

"Not as much as I would have liked," he said, forcing himself to smile. "But then you seemed quite at ease with letting a man disrobe you. You must have had plenty of practice."

44

Compromised

She advanced on him. "Never in my life has a man been so crude touching me as you did that night in the garden."

"So you've succeeded in convincing all your suitors that you're made of ice?" John's voice was husky, and he'd barely got the words out coherently. Her breasts were only hidden behind scraps of silk that outlined her nipples and revealed the shadowed valley in between. His arousal became almost painful. It didn't matter to his cock that she was angry and miserable.

"My suitors were gentlemen," she said, stalking away from him.

He almost choked at the sight of her backside, which he wanted to grab in two handfuls to pull her up against him. "I've brought you a wedding gift," he managed to say.

She made no response, only sat down in a chair before a little table littered with her combs and perfumes. When he sat across from her, she slid back farther in her chair, as if she were afraid to touch him. And a little devil inside him made him lean even closer. He held out the pouch, and she reluctantly took it.

She opened the drawstring and withdrew a small hand mirror, its handle twined with silver and gold.

"It was my grandmother's," he said, glancing at the dressing table, with its fancier mirror.

Elizabeth set it on the table behind her, then looked up at him with wintry eyes. "Thank you for the gift."

"Ah, good breeding wins out," he said, trying to smile and make the best of their situation. He took one of her soft hands in his, but she pulled away and stood up. Her night rail brushed across his skin, and the scent of her perfume made him once more think of the secrets of her body he'd only begun to explore that dark night. He could not stop the memory of her mouth hot and eager beneath his. He closed his eyes.

"I just have one question for you," she said.

John turned in his chair, letting his arm dangle over the back, trying to appear unaffected. She was certainly not afraid of him, and for that he was grateful.

"All you needed to do was tell one small lie and say we hadn't kissed," she said, her voice cold and steady. "Why did you not? What other reason could there be except for my dowry? You were obviously looking to marry, considering that you'd brought a gift for the lucky, chosen woman all the way from Yorkshire."

The last was said with such sarcasm that he barely held back a smile, even though he knew she meant to offend him. "I told you I came to London to find a wife. I did not need to compromise a woman to persuade her to marry me. What happened between us was unplanned, although certainly enjoyable."

She rolled her eyes.

"I would have said nothing, but once the gallant Sir Ralph came forward—I take it he is another of your spurned suitors—I was not about to lie. I could have easily gone home, my reputation intact, perhaps strengthened, and you would have been ruined."

She stalked back towards him, and again her lovely body made thinking difficult.

"Are you saying you told the truth to protect me?" she demanded.

"Yes. For that and honor, of course."

"Honor? Forcing a woman to marry you is honorable?"

Compromised

"It was your father doing the forcing, and believe me, I was hardly overjoyed. But I could not leave you behind to suffer for what we'd done."

"How noble of you," she said, blinking back tears. "But although I went outside with you that night, I had no idea what was involved, what you'd—what we'd—"

The tear that slipped down her cheek made him stand up and draw her into his arms, though she remained unyielding.

"I didn't think about your innocence that night," he whispered into her ear. "I'm sorry."

Elizabeth stood in his warm embrace and listened to his apology. She could even hear the beat of his heart, steady and strong. For just a moment, she almost believed he was sincere, but then against her belly, she felt the hard reminder of his desire.

She stumbled away from him. "Will you say anything to get me into bed?" she cried, dashing away her foolish tears.

"I cannot help how my body reacts to your beauty."

"Is that your only excuse for compromising me, marrying me—"

"Elizabeth—"

"No! I will not do it! I don't care what you expect from me, but this is one thing I control."

He came toward her, and even though she backed up until her legs hit the bed, she refused to be afraid of him.

"Elizabeth, if you believe that, then you are lucky to be married to me."

"Lucky!"

"Any other man would put you on your back, spread your legs—"

She winced at his crudity.

"—and take your maidenhead, as is a husband's right. But perhaps this is your strategy. You are flaunting your body—"

"Flaunting!"

"—in hopes that I'll force myself on you, and prove myself some kind of monster in your eyes. Then you'd have something to complain to your father about."

"I would scream before I let you touch me!"

"Maybe they'll think you're screaming with pleasure."

His voice had dropped into that low range that did something strange to her insides. She could only blink at him. Scream with pleasure? Women did that?

Then she remembered being in his arms, alone in the garden, his hands stroking, caressing—and the embarrassing sounds she'd made. She blushed and turned away from him, only to find the bed spread out before her.

She stared at the turned-down coverlet and said very firmly, "The only way I will lie with you tonight is if you force me."

Behind her he said nothing, and she risked looking over her shoulder. He watched her with those unfathomable dark eyes.

"I won't allow this marriage to be annulled," he said softly, dangerously. "But I am willing to wait until your...sensibilities adjust, but I won't promise not to persuade you."

"Persuade!"

"And I will keep at it until you succumb."

He reached out and although she flinched, she could do nothing else because the bed was right behind her. He slid his warm fingers down her neck, then along the lace neckline of her night rail. Holding her breath, she prayed he could not tell how rapidly her heart was beating, how much her body was betraying her, melting beneath his caress. She was so weak, she would need little persuasion at all.

His thumb rubbed across her nipple, and she gave an involuntary shudder as a spasm of pleasure rocked her.

"You're easy to gaze upon, Elizabeth."

She licked her lips and watched his hand cup her breast and gently squeeze. In a weak voice, she tried again to dissuade him. "I have scars—big, ugly ones."

"Well, it certainly was dark in that garden, so I might have missed it. Let me see."

He flicked the night rail off her shoulder, and it bared her breast before she could catch the silk and cover herself.

"You promised not to force me," she whispered, and her gaze caught and held his.

After a moment, he stepped back. "I won't."

"Then where will you sleep?"

He gave her a disbelieving look. "Right here."

He unbelted his tunic and lifted it over his head to reveal a white shirt. As he untied his codpiece, she sat back heavily on the bed, but thankfully he was wearing linen braies that covered his hips. He dropped his boots and hose to the floor, and she noticed that his bare legs were hairy.

When he pulled the shirt over his head, she almost stopped breathing. His chest was broad and sculpted with muscle, scattered with brown hair that narrowed down over his stomach. The arms which had lifted her, held her, were even more impressive bare. If all men were made like

49

him, it was a wonder women weren't being compromised all the time.

"I have scars, too," John said, a grin transforming his face. "Want to come and see?"

She shook her head quickly. "I can see just fine from here."

Elizabeth knew she shouldn't even be looking, that he'd lose much of his power if only she'd ignore him.

But…how to ignore a man whose presence, whose very maleness made the room seem smaller around him? Even the few scars across his chest and arms were impressive.

"Did you not bring something to wear?" she asked.

"I don't wear anything to bed, and certainly not on my wedding night."

He dropped the braies to the floor and stood before her naked. She couldn't stop her eyes from widening as she looked at his large…manhood—she didn't even know the right word. It seemed to point accusingly at her. She was not so innocent that she didn't know where that was supposed to go, regardless of her mother's cryptic words. But she had thought it would be…smaller. He walked toward her, and she couldn't stop staring at it.

"I don't suppose this persuaded you," he said, so close to her she had to lean back on her hands not to touch him.

She looked up his body at his face, to find him no longer smiling.

"Certainly not," she said, relieved when her voice didn't shake.

He crawled onto the bed beside her. "That's a shame. You don't know what you're missing."

"Is that a boast?"

Compromised

"I don't need to boast." He stretched out his long body until his feet almost hung over the end. His manhood lay large and flat on his stomach.

"Aren't you going to cover yourself?"

"Nay, it's rather warm in here, is it not?"

She could hardly deny that, not when her skin felt moist and clammy. She was flustered and tense—and fascinated enough to want to stare at his body, even touch it. She stood up quickly before she could make a fool of herself.

"Lie down, Elizabeth."

She looked wildly about the room, knowing he wouldn't allow her to escape. He'd promised not to force her—but he hadn't promised not to touch her. She shivered.

"Cold?" he asked, and she heard amusement in his voice. "I wouldn't have thought so in this heat, but I promise I'll keep you warm."

"No, thank you."

She blew out all the candles leaving the room in complete darkness. She should feel relieved not to have to stare at his nakedness, but she was left with the worry of what he might be doing.

After perching on the bed, she lay stiffly to her side, keeping as close to the edge as possible. When he didn't move or say anything, she allowed herself to relax the tiniest bit.

His arm suddenly caught her and pulled her closer to him. She gave a little shriek, trying desperately to push him away.

"Elizabeth, I won't have you falling off the bed. Now go to sleep."

He withdrew from her, but now she worried that he'd touch her again. She lay wide awake, even after she heard his soft snore.

~oOo~

John came awake before dawn and lay still in the gray darkness. The air was warm and humid, and he had remained uncovered through the night. Of course he was also kept warm by Elizabeth, who in her sleep persisted in cuddling up against him. Even now, she lay with her back pressed against his side.

He stared at the canopy over the bed and sighed. At first he'd almost been angry. It had taken a long time for her to fall asleep, and her small movements kept him awake—along with the cock-stand which had seemed to grow harder with her every sigh. When she'd finally slept, she'd rolled against him and snuggled in for the duration. Twice he'd pushed her gently away, especially when he could feel her pointed nipples in his back, or when she'd thrown her leg right over his groin.

But John was awake now, and she lay against him so provocatively, and hadn't he promised he'd keep trying to seduce her? Carefully, he turned on his side and slid behind her, molding his thighs to hers, her buttocks cradling his erection. He was so hard, even a few thrusts like this would be enough.

But certainly not satisfying. He settled his arm around her waist, feeling the smoothness of the silk as he splayed his hand across her soft stomach. He hesitated, then slid his hand up her ribcage and cupped one generous breast. She stirred in her sleep, squirming her hips. Taking a ragged breath at the delicious assault, he buried his face in her hair.

Compromised

He told himself to stop, that in the end he would be the frustrated one, but instead he caressed her nipples through her night rail, rubbing them to hard peaks between his fingers. She moaned softly, moving restlessly, and he rubbed his hips against hers from behind.

Pushing her hair out of the way, he nibbled her earlobe, and let his fingers trail down her stomach between her closed thighs. As she shuddered and moaned again, he probed as deeply as the silk let him, rubbing against the curls over her woman's mound, tickling at the nub that was the center of her passion.

Chapter 5

Elizabeth came awake feeling afire, achy and almost feverish. What was wrong with her? And then she felt John's body behind her, his arms encircling her, his mouth kissing her ear, her cheek. One arm was beneath her, his fingers tormenting her breast, while with his other hand he pulled up her night rail. Every inch of her skin felt alive with sensation as the silk slid against her, and she was frightened by how much she wanted his hand between her legs.

She knew she should stop him, but she was held immobile by the mounting flames which seemed to engulf her body. Her breath came in frantic gasps. When her night rail was finally bunched at her waist, he sank his fingers into her curls, rubbing and stroking until she cried out at the wondrous pleasure mounting in her.

Then he suddenly stopped, withdrawing his hands but not his body, leaving her lost, aching. She froze as he whispered in her ear.

"I am too much a gentleman to force myself on you. Should I continue?"

Mortified, Elizabeth rolled away and pulled the night rail down her thighs and sat up.

"You did that on purpose!" she whispered, pushing her hair out of her eyes to glare at him.

Compromised

With his back to her, he pulled on his braies and hose, and she wondered if his codpiece could possibly cover what he now kept hidden from her.

"I told you from the beginning that I would try to seduce you."

John faced her bare-chested, frowning his anger, and she was reluctantly impressed by how magnificent he looked.

"Since you spent all night pressing against me," he said between gritted teeth, "I felt free to take some liberties."

He paused, and his voice became deeper, deadly to her self-control.

"I could come back to bed. Are you asking me to?"

For a moment, she almost opened her arms to him, so desperate was she to find out what would end this dreadful ache. His brown eyes burned into her, and when they dropped down her body she could have gladly stripped off her night rail.

She was coming so easily under his control, she thought bitterly. He wasn't the husband for her, and she didn't want this marriage. Though he said he would not allow her to annul it, there might be other ways around him. Raising her chin, she gave him the haughtiest look she could muster.

"Thank you for the invitation, but I decline," she said coolly.

His slow grin made her knees shaky as she stood.

"Suit yourself, my lady. I'll be waiting. All you have to do is ask."

She turned her back on him, and wanted to cover her ears when he chuckled.

After he'd gone, she wrote the letter she'd been composing in her mind since this horrible wedding disaster began. She didn't want Lord Wyndham to think she was suddenly in love with another man, not after his lordship had been pursuing her so sweetly. She begged his forgiveness, writing that she was unhappy with both the marriage and the idea of living so far away in Yorkshire.

She reread it again. Would Lord Wyndham understand that she had withheld her favors from John, that there might still be a chance for her and his lordship to be together after an annulment?

She almost felt guilty—until she remembered John's promise to seduce her, to make her his wife in every way. Wasn't that the same thing as forcing her?

Before she could change her mind, she sealed the letter with wax, then had her maid deliver it.

~oOo~

John was mildly surprised when Elizabeth's parents did not argue with his plans to depart the day after the wedding. It was customary to spend a few days with the bride's parents, and he might have relented had they asked him to stay, but they didn't. Elizabeth took the news stoically, her face pale and composed. When he asked about her friend, Katherine, she'd looked about to cry, and only frantically shook her head. It was Nicholas who told John that Katharine was still unaccounted for, her family uncommunicative. The earl had told Elizabeth that she was a married woman now, and had no business interfering in whatever problems the Berkeley family was having.

Not very sympathetic, John thought, and not very helpful for a peaceful start to their married life.

Compromised

When he returned to their home at midday with horses, two carts, and hired servants, he found a multitude of trunks holding Elizabeth's garments. Dismayed but not surprised, he had the servants load the carts as best they could, but the final two trunks interfered with where the maidservants—and his bride—would be sitting. He was tempted to toss both trunks, but decided to let her choose how comfortable she would be on the journey.

After a small midday dinner that John felt hardly suited a farewell to the only daughter of the household, he stood outside near the carts, and watched Elizabeth and her mother, who was still dressed as if in mourning, descend the stairs.

"Did your father already say his good-byes?" John asked, reaching for Elizabeth's hand at the final few steps.

She ignored his help. "He was called away to court."

He could tell she was making every effort to control her voice, while he made no effort at all to hide his angry scowl. Her father seemed to deliberately reminded her she was a disappointment every chance he got. John was beginning to realize that his wife would fare much better with his family—if she would let herself.

Elizabeth turned to her mother and hugged her hard, and though she whispered to keep her words from him, he had excellent hearing.

"Mother, do not worry for me. John is not a cruel man. I swear that somehow I will make you proud of me."

Though Lady Chelmsford continued to cry, she did not hold her daughter for long. When she raised imploring eyes to his, he smiled encouragingly, then guided the trembling Elizabeth to their pack train of horses and carts.

"Would you care to ride in a cart or upon a horse?" he asked.

She only stiffened, then looked at the trunks piled on the cart and overflowing to interfere with a passenger's feet.

"How am I supposed to find comfort like this?" she demanded in a quiet voice.

"Leave the trunks home, and you will not have a problem."

"I cannot do that! I need all these things, especially in the uncivilized north."

"Uncivilized?" He flashed her a grin. "We shall see who is uncivilized."

The maids rode in the carts, but Elizabeth elected to ride. He suggested she ride pillion behind him, but instead she mounted her horse astride, leaving him reluctantly impressed.

Before he mounted, she gave him a hesitant, beseeching look. "Might we stop at the Earl of Durham's manor? To see if Katherine has returned home?"

He'd meant to travel as far as possible before making camp for the night, but he understood Elizabeth's worry. "Very well. But we cannot remain long."

Biting her lip, she only nodded her gratitude.

At the earl's manor home on the banks of the Thames, John was forbidden entrance by the two guards. When he turned back to inform Elizabeth, she was already sliding off her horse. She meant to march past him, but he caught her arm.

" 'Tis of no use," he said gently.

She shook him off. "I am the daughter of the Earl of Chelmsford. They have to listen to me."

Compromised

He didn't try to stop her. She walked toward the guards with her head held high, and John saw the two men glance at each other once in silent communication, before fixing their sober gazes on Elizabeth.

"Gentlemen, Lady Katherine is my dearest friend. Surely you have seen me visit here a thousand times. Let me pass, so that I may comfort her in whatever sickness or tragedy has befallen the family."

"We cannot, milady," said the one guard.

"We have our orders," said the other.

"You will not dare to stop me!"

John thought she meant her voice to sound determined, but it quavered with her worry for her friend. "Elizabeth, come with me."

"No, something is wrong. I need to help."

The two guards only crossed their long pikes against her.

John took her shoulders from behind, and for a moment, he thought she would fight him. But all stiffness left her shoulders, and she bowed her head.

"Katherine," she whispered forlornly.

He couldn't help but feel sorry for her, separated from her family, off to a new life, and now this worry for her friend. He led her away, watching as she kept her chin high, though her lips trembled.

"The family might simply be ill, and not wish to start a panic," he murmured.

"She would tell me," Elizabeth insisted.

"And if they would not permit it?"

She shook her head. "Something is truly wrong, I know it."

"Then trust Nicholas to find you some answers."

Though she mounted without assistance, she turned her head away from him, and he saw her shoulders shake with a silent sob. He briefly closed his eyes in pain, and felt pity for his new wife.

During the first few days of their journey, John rode beside the carts, and Elizabeth alternated between her horse and the hard wooden cart bench. It was dreadfully hot, and she wore layers of garments. Two hired maidservants clutched the bouncing cart, and he felt sorry for all three of them. He didn't think being miserable would help Elizabeth in the long run, but he reluctantly understood her problems. Too many things out of her control had happened in the last few days.

The first two nights when her pavilion was erected, she remained inside with her maids, rather than sit with him near the fire. He never had a chance to touch her hand, let alone attempt to seduce her. He decided that things were going to be different the next night.

~oOo~

Carts were never a comfortable ride, and the farther north they traveled the highway, the more they bounced from hole to hole, jarring Elizabeth's backbone, and once sending her across the maidservant's lap. Her thighs and backside were aching from long hours on horseback. The heat was oppressive and stifling. They'd seen beggars on the road, even young children, which made her want to cry. They'd been stuck behind long pack trains of merchants carting their wares between towns and villages. The only good thing she could say was that it hadn't rained.

As dusk began to descend, she breathed a sigh of relief, even though it meant another night encamped in near wilderness. To her surprise, the road they were traveling smoothed out as they approached a village. They stopped in the Market Square, where she saw the hanging sign for an inn, an angel with a flaming sword. The inn was several stories tall with a passageway beneath the second story that led into a courtyard, where above them each floor had open galleries.

John glanced at her with satisfaction. "Will this do for the night, wife?"

She flinched at being addressed with her new title, but didn't complain, only gave a quiet groan as she dismounted. She kept a hand on the saddle as her legs threatened to collapse beneath her. She'd never stayed at an inn before. When they traveled between her father's manors and castles, they stayed with other nobleman, or at monasteries.

John guided her and her maidservants inside, while the men saw to the horses. In a low timber-ceilinged room on the ground floor, a half dozen men crowded at tables before a large stone fireplace. Everyone looked at her, some called out ribald greetings, but John was large and menacing as he faced them down.

The innkeeper had a dormitory room for the servants, and a private chamber for them. But when the innkeeper's wife opened the door, and Elizabeth caught the smell of stale rushes on the floor, hiding who knew what beneath, she gave the woman a pleasant smile.

"We can wait in your public room while you sweep out the rushes and lay down new. Please also replace the bedding."

"Mistress, ye get the chamber as is," the woman said, lisping slightly because of several missing teeth.

Elizabeth continued to speak politely. "You may address me as 'my lady.' If you wish to receive good payment for your services, please make the room presentable. Come, Lord Malory."

She realized she was ordering John about, but he smiled at her as if she amused him. Ridiculous man. She wasn't his entertainment.

He put up a hand as if he could read her mind. "I am simply impressed."

As they went back down the tight staircase, she said over her shoulder, "I have dealt with servants my entire life. Firm politeness works best. My father would never accept the truth of that and his disdain only encouraged frightened servants into doing poor work."

"Very true."

As they emerged into the smoky public room, she glanced at John. "Have you worked with servants?"

He looked like he was trying not to laugh. "I have."

She took a deep breath, narrowing her eyes at him. "So you *have* servants?"

"You're actually asking me about myself?"

She turned away from his sarcasm. She didn't want to talk to him at all.

He purchased her and the other servants meat pies, and by the time their bellies were full, their chambers were ready. The male servants filed into their dormitory next door, and to Elizabeth's surprise, John barred the way of the women, who'd been about to enter the private bedchamber.

"I will see to my wife tonight," he said.

Compromised

He was speaking with firm politeness, just as she'd told him worked best with servants. And now she didn't like it—in fact, it made her downright nervous.

"I need their assistance," she pointed out. Was that nervousness in her voice?

He ignored her and continued speaking to the women. "There is a small chamber on the far side of the dormitory. You may sleep separate from the men."

The women hurried away and Elizabeth frowned as she watched them go. They seemed far too happy to be relieved of their duties. When she turned to glare up at John, he was studying her with eyes full of triumph and far too much smoldering interest. She remembered how he'd awakened her the morning after her wedding, setting afire her skin, making every thought of protest disappear. She could not allow that to happen again. He'd gotten his wife, but not yet the dowry he wanted. She wasn't going to make it easy for him.

She stepped haughtily into their chamber—and came to a stop. There was a bathing tub set before the hearth, steam rising from it. Several extra buckets of water remained nearby. On the table were set a stack of linens and a pot of what must be soap.

"I did not order this," she said, trying to tamp down the panic in her voice.

"You don't wish to bathe after two days on the road?"

She heard him close the door and whirled to find him leaning against it, eyeing her.

"You ordered this."

"I have a way with servants, too." He moved past her and trailed his fingers through the water. "Ahh."

Oh God, it looked wondrous. But—"If you leave, I will bathe."

"I will not leave my wife alone in a dangerous inn."

"You brought me to a dangerous inn?"

"Every accommodation is dangerous."

"Not the palaces of my father's friends."

"An earl has access to places and people that a baron does not, I'm afraid."

"So you will not allow your wife to bathe," she continued.

"So now you're my wife?" he asked in a low voice.

She lifted her chin and said nothing.

"Very well, I'll stand outside the door. But do not take long, because I, too, need to bathe, and I don't wish the water to be freezing."

"You—you will use the water when I'm finished?" she demanded. "Send for more."

"It took a large bribe to even arrange this. Inns for the lower classes offer a basin to wash in, not a bathing tub. We are lucky." He looked down her body, frowning. "Now I'll have to listen to you bathing. Perhaps it would be better for me if the water *was* cold when it's my turn."

"I beg your pardon?"

"Never mind."

Someone knocked at the door.

"I told one of the servants to bring you up a trunk." He strode past her and opened the door.

"I wish you would have given me the choice."

Elizabeth practically fell back as her oversize trunk came through. After placing it in a corner, the servants bowed to her and left.

Compromised

"I imagine this trunk will do," Elizabeth said, her mind dwelling on a bath and clean clothes. "Do you not need a trunk?"

"A have a saddle bag." He gestured with his chin toward the table.

She hadn't even noticed. She was glad not to have to talk to him, as she knelt beside her trunk and pulled out another smock and gown.

"I'll leave you to your bath."

She heard the door close behind him. She didn't waste any more time, just began to disrobe with great haste. Soon she was sitting in the bathing tub, closing her eyes in bliss. It was nothing like the padded deep tubs back in London, where she could submerge herself, but at least it let the water rise to rib height. She spent a moment relaxing, the heat soothing her sore muscles, before she thought it best to begin washing. And then she realized she hadn't set anything she needed nearby.

No sooner did she rise out of the water and reach for the soap, than she heard, "Are you done?" called through the door.

"No!"

With a facecloth, she washed herself. The soap smelled plain, like what one would use cleaning dishes, but she didn't care. Next she soaped her hair. There was a handy bucket nearby with fresh water to pour over her head and sluice away the suds.

"Now are you done?"

"Not yet!" She had to reach for the linen, which she'd also forgotten to keep nearby.

"Go dress behind the screen," he called. "I'm coming in."

Grumbling under her breath, she wrapped the linen around herself, stepped from the tub and slipped behind the screen with her garments. "I'm finished."

When the door opened and closed, she peeked out. He nodded at her and began to unbuckle his belt.

"I don't mind if you watch me bathe," he said, a half smile teasing her.

"Do you think to intimidate me?"

He shrugged and set his sheathed sword and dagger on the table with a jarring jangle that rattled her nerves. He looked at her as if he thought she'd be too frightened to get another view of his nakedness. She glared at him, but didn't retreat, though she kept her body behind the screen. She didn't know what she was trying to accomplish except to show him that he couldn't cow her. It was a silent game between them, to see who would back down first.

Next he began to work on the buckles and straps of the plated brigandine he'd worn to protect his chest on the journey. He looked at the tub as if it were his salvation.

"A good wife would scrub her man's back."

"I will not be your good wife."

"Such a shame. Luckily, I've been a single man for many a year and know how to bathe myself. I'm wondering if you've ever done so without a servant waiting to hand you the soap or your linens."

He was far too close to the truth. Had he been spying on her? But no, she'd watched the door closely. "My personal habits are none of your business."

"They are now."

Compromised

His voice was deep and full of a meaning she didn't want to face. He put his brigandine in a corner of the chamber, and removed the belt that cinched his tunic. Was she going to have to watch him disrobe every night and remember how he'd loosened her clothes that dark night in the garden?

She had to dress. What good was a challenge if she stood around wearing a linen and giving him ideas? She ducked her head back behind the screen.

"Coward," he called.

"I am wet and nearly naked. I need to dress."

She thought he groaned, but she didn't want to know why. His clothing continued to make enticing rustling noises in time with hers.

"I hope you appreciate that you bathed first," he said. "A gentleman allows his wife the clean water—or so my brother has always told me."

"What are you talking about?"

She heard the slosh of water, and imagined him sinking up to his waist.

"I have a brother," he continued, "not that you asked."

"And when were we supposed to converse?" she asked dryly.

"We've had two days on the road, and you've remained stubbornly silent."

"I have every right to keep to myself," she whispered.

He might not have been able to hear her, but he seemed to understand, for he didn't ask her to repeat herself.

But did she have that right? Every man was in charge of his wife; she'd been raised seeing that example daily. A man could beat his wife with impunity—not that she'd seen her father do that. And if her mother on occasion cried alone in her bedchamber, Elizabeth had always assumed they'd quarreled. They were not the happiest couple she'd ever seen.

She'd hoped for better in her own marriage, and instead she'd allowed herself to be trapped by lust and stupidity, forced into marriage with a stranger for all time.

Oh God, how could she even complain, when Katherine was out there somewhere, in trouble? She just *knew* something dire had happened.

She was distracted by sounds of the water moving, and to her shame, she imagined him washing himself.

"What is your brother's name?" she asked, to distract herself. She put on a clean smock to sleep in. It was made of far sturdier, less revealing fabric than her night rail.

"William. He is younger than I, but married and the father of many children."

Surprised, she thoughtlessly stepped out from behind the screen—and found the sight of his chest above the tub, glistening with moisture, strangely arousing. It was just a chest. What was wrong with her?

"Done with hiding?" he asked.

"I was not hiding. I was dressing."

He'd sunk into the bathing tub as much as he could, so his bent knees stuck up, and the water lapped at his chest. It should be awkward, but he looked at her with half closed eyes, a faint smile on his face, as relaxed as any man she'd ever seen. She shivered, aroused and intrigued and disappointed in herself.

But there was still a light of challenge in his eyes, and she was too ready to accept. She didn't turn away, just lifted her chin and tried to pretend she was unaffected. He chuckled—he actually chuckled! She'd never heard a light sound of amusement from him and she didn't know what to think about it.

She went past him toward the bed, ignoring the moist heat of the tub and the lure of the naked man. What was she supposed to do with herself?

"Ahh," John said.

Without thinking she looked again, just catching the view from the back as he rose to his feet. Water ran down his torso and buttocks, gleaming in trails as it meandered along muscle and bone.

He glanced at her over his shoulder. "The water isn't too dirty."

"Do you expect me to believe that is a compliment?"

He chuckled. Again.

She whirled away, folded her arms over chest, and realized she was staring at the bed. Pretending to meander to the window, she leaned against the sill and looked out on the moonlit night, taking in a deep breath of air that didn't smell like damp skin and kitchen soap. They should be terrible smells, but…they weren't.

When the servants came to remove the bathing tub, Elizabeth ducked behind the screen until they were gone. She listened to John's easy conversation with them as he asked about the road north and how the weather had been. He did not seem to be a man given to wild excesses of emotions. Even when provoked, he never seemed out of control, just relaxed and confident.

She'd given him far too many reasons to feel confident he could have what he wanted from her: the security of her dowry, a woman in his bed, heirs. She'd been a tool of her father's, and now she'd be used by her husband. It seemed unfair and frustrating and depressing. Why had she not understood a woman's fate when she was younger? She'd seen Katherine ignored by her betrothed for *years*, watched her feel neglected and inferior, though her friend was always pleasant and resigned.

Had Elizabeth thought she herself would be different, that she could simply snap her fingers and the man she wanted would fall into line, showering her with praise and gifts and letting her do whatever she wanted? She'd been so naïve.

Taking a deep breath, she tried to be appear unperturbed as she emerged from behind the screen. John was taking up practically the whole bed, the blankets loosely around his waist, his chest uncovered. Hands on her hips, she glared at him.

He slid a few inches nearer the edge. "You have to sleep closest to the wall. Unless you want to defend us from an intruder."

She rolled her eyes. The chamber was small enough that she'd have to crawl across him to reach the interior of the bed.

"Sit up," she ordered.

"You're not very polite."

"Please," she added coldly.

He sat up, shaking his head. "I spend good money at an inn to please you, and this is the behavior that results."

The twinge of guilt she felt angered her, so she said nothing, just climbed into the bed behind him, hugged the wall as much as she could, and told herself to relax.

She could hear him breathing. It was too warm for a fire, so when he blew out the candle, the darkness was only relieved by the flickering torches that lit the courtyard below their window. She remembered what had happened on their wedding night, how she'd woken up cuddled against him. Surely it was too hot for her to make that mistake again, even in sleep. She didn't slide beneath the blanket because her legs already felt sweaty. She wasn't about to pull her smock up to her thighs, as she would when in bed alone. She could only imagine John would take that as an invitation. And she wasn't giving in, not yet. She was still so angry that her life was turning out to be like nothing she'd imagined.

Not that it was totally John's fault. She could admit that to herself. But once she'd...given herself to him, he would have everything he wanted. It didn't seem fair, when she was losing her entire way of life.

She sounded childish, even in her own head, and let out a sigh. To distract herself, she added up what she thought he'd spent for this night at the inn. Numbers had a way of calming her. Her father would give her spending money, and she prided herself on allocating it for fabric or notions, leaving some for the occasional play or book.

But numbers weren't helping her sleep that night.

"Do you have any sisters?" she asked.

"No."

"Is your mother still alive?"

"Yes. She will be pleased to meet you."

Elizabeth barely kept from snorting. What mother would be pleased to meet the strange woman her son had been forced to marry?

"You had to come to London to find a wife—are there none in Yorkshire?"

"None I fancied."

"None with a wealthy dowry," she countered.

"Do you know nothing about York? 'Tis a wealthy town with many heiresses."

"But none that suited you," she said sarcastically. "Or none that would *have* you."

"Believe what you will," he said, rolling onto his side away from her. "You'll know the truth when we arrive home."

Home. An ache spread out from her chest, and she had to concentrate hard to keep her tears at bay. His home—where she'd be seen as the unwanted interloper, where all would find out their beloved John had been forced to marry, where she'd have no one to turn to for comfort or support.

Chapter 6

Elizabeth spent a restless night, her muscles stiff, trying to stop thinking and worrying—and trying not to touch John. It was as if her unconscious self was drawn to him, and she was disgusted by such weakness of both body and will.

Exhausted, she fell into a deep sleep in the darkest part of the night. Later, as if from beneath the peaceful surface of a pond, she began to surface, feeling comfortable and warm, even content. She felt the most gentle caresses along her arms and shoulders, easing the stiffness, making her want to purr like a cat. Her mind floating, she let it go on, though some faraway part of her knew there was a reason to stop it. The touches moved lower, along her hips and bare legs, and she squirmed deliciously. The comfort and peacefulness were changing now, as her skin seemed to hum with rising eagerness. She wanted those caresses, resisted the urge to focus on why this might be wrong. She felt like she'd indulged in too much wine and was incapable of rational thought—or she was resisting it.

The first caress of her breast made her moan, but still she did not open her eyes, resisting reality, resisting the buzz of concern way at the back of her mind. This felt too good, after days of feeling so bad. Languid, she let him knead and cup her breasts through her smock, teasing her nipples into aching points. Such sensual delight felt too good to be wrong, and she heard herself moan when his caresses stopped.

But she didn't have to wait long, as he began a slow meander up her bare legs, light, teasing, gentle touches that seemed to set her afire, the higher they went. Behind her knee was particularly sensitive, and her inner thighs burned with impatience for him to do more. And he did, sliding her smock higher until she knew her lower body was nude. Instead of yanking on her garments or rolling away, she separated her legs and fisted her hands in the bed sheets, begging with her body for what she could not say with words, not yet. She wouldn't even open her eyes and look at him.

When he placed a gentle kiss low on her belly, she shuddered. He reached beneath her smock and began to play with her bare breast, rubbing her nipples, pinching them, soothing them, even as he blew on the curls at the juncture of her thighs. She bit her lip to keep from saying his name in desperation.

When he placed a kiss right *there*, she practically came off the bed with shock and a dark eagerness she didn't even recognize in herself. Oh, but she did—she was transforming into the wanton woman of that night in the garden, who wanted whatever wild, reckless thing he could do to her.

He kissed her deeper and deeper, then his tongue stroked and swirled the little nub, and she flung an arm over her eyes as if she couldn't bear to look—or bear to have him see her face as what he did moved through her in a hot surge of passion that took her away from herself, made her feel like a desperate creature. His hand caressed her breasts, his mouth suckled, rising passion engulfed her

74

body, taking her higher and higher until the most amazing release crashed down over her, leaving her gasping and spent.

For several long minutes, nothing else happened. She could hear his quick breathing, but he didn't touch her. She felt the bed move, and she braced herself for him to climb atop her, as her mother had said. But it didn't happen.

At last she opened her eyes, only to find him sitting on the edge of the bed with his back to her, his head in his hands, the muscles of his bare back rippling with each ragged breath.

"John? Did I do something wrong?"

"Nay, my God, you are perfect," he whispered hoarsely. But he still didn't look at her.

She looked at herself—at the rumpled smock, her naked hips, and she burned with embarrassment remembering where he'd just been.

"But I won't make you my wife this night," he said.

"I *am* your wife."

"Not in the way it most matters. You accepted what I just did to you, Elizabeth, but you didn't want me to do it. You don't want *me*."

She didn't know what to say to that. He was right. She didn't want this life, felt more and more lost the farther they got from London and the only people she knew. She hadn't wanted to grant him the gift of her virginity, and now he wasn't taking it.

"Then why did you…" She trailed off, not even certain what to call the things he'd done to her.

"Because I couldn't resist showing you what we could have together." He glanced over his shoulder and met her wide eyes with a smoldering gaze. "There's more, Elizabeth, and I'll make you want it so badly that you'll beg for me to take you."

She wanted to become defensive again, to be angry, but he stood up, naked, and she watched as he walked behind the screen, not bothering to hide his arousal from her. Then she yanked her smock down as if covering herself would cover the memories. It didn't work that way.

~oOo~

Elizabeth rode her horse much of the day, and spoke little to John unless he asked her a question. Her thoughts about her role as his wife continued to squirm around inside her head until she felt dizzy. When they made camp that night, she fell asleep quickly after her poor night's rest lying at John's side at the inn.

In the last hour before dawn, something beside the heat woke her. She lay still on her lumpy pallet, hoping it was just one of the maids snoring, but knowing in a cold, chill way that it was not. She could no longer see the bright shadows of the fire on the walls of the pavilion, though she distinctly remembered John ordering the guards to keep a fire going at all times.

When she heard rustling out in their camp, she wondered if they were being invaded by wild animals—which John had assured her the fire would keep away. Why was she worrying? For a man who'd never been to London, never been to court, John had proved himself more than capable of command. The farther from civilization they traveled, he seemed to grow larger, more expansive, while she felt small and lost.

Yet he was the first one she thought of now that she was frightened—not her father, not her suitor Lord

Compromised

Wyndham. The noises outside had grown louder, and she heard flesh striking flesh, and a man's moan. As she awoke her maids, she hushed their voices, whispering that they had to dress quickly.

There was a call of warning, and then the shouts of men as they fought. The maids cried, but Elizabeth was trying not to. She was afraid to look outside, and afraid to sit there unknowing. With shaking hands, she parted the canvas flap and peered out.

Men she didn't know had invaded the camp. There were fistfights, swords clashing, and desperate shouting. Eventually there were fewer and fewer men, as John's guards were slipping away into the forest. How could they desert the lord who'd paid them with what little money he had?

She turned to look after the maids, only to find them gone, the pavilion torn where they'd taken a knife to it. Elizabeth was tempted to join them, but she didn't know anything about forests and wild animals. Her only safety was John, who was fighting for his life—and who'd put her in this terrible situation in the first place, she reminded herself.

But what if he died? What if she was left at the mercy of such barbarians?

When she looked back out, John was running toward the tent, and a feeling of relief brought tears to her eyes. He wasn't dead.

For a strange moment, she noticed everything in the growing light of dawn—the surprised faces of the thieves, the blood that trickled from a cut at John's temple. Then he grabbed her and shoved her behind him, brandishing his sword at the thieves menacingly.

"Just take whatever goods you want," he said. "But hurry, because this is a well-traveled road, and someone is sure to come this way soon."

Elizabeth felt her throat closing up, just when she might need to scream. The men looked at her contemplatively, as if she were a side of beef at market day. My God, did John think they might want her?

There was a tense moment of silence, and she was frozen with fear and anxiety, wondering what they would do. Her hands dug into John's waist as she clung to him, pressing her face against his back.

"Leave 'er," said a tall, spare man, who seemed to be the leader. "Take everythin' else."

With a cry, she retreated into the tent, trying to save some of her belongings, desperately pulling on her farthingale to hold up her skirts. She thought of how she'd examined John's purchases for the journey, relieved that at least he'd been prepared to take care of her. She'd often tried to alleviate her boredom by estimating what he'd spent—she knew what things cost. But if it was all taken away, what would they do?

John grabbed her as the tent was invaded and thrust her out into the trees.

"Do something!" she pleaded, looking over her shoulder. "They're taking our things!"

"I did do something—I negotiated and saved you from them. And they're taking my things, too," he added dryly, pulling her deeper into the dense foliage, "including the horses and carts."

"But surely the servants will return for us."

Compromised

"They're London-bred, Elizabeth. They didn't fancy Yorkshire, let alone being robbed in the wilderness. I think we've seen the last of them."

She felt numb with shock, unable to imagine being abandoned by servants. Soon they were alone in the dappled sunrise, shaded by the encroaching Sherwood Forest. They had nothing but the garments they were wearing, no way to protect themselves from predators human or otherwise. The world suddenly seemed enormous, and herself tiny and frail.

"What are we going to do?" she whispered in a daze.

"We're going to walk, of course."

"To the next town? Will we find horses there?"

"We've no money left to buy them. Unless…"

He suddenly leaned toward her and snatched at her hair. She batted him away, knowing she was overreacting, but unable to stop herself.

"Easy, my lady," he murmured patiently, which made her feel worse. "You have a jeweled hair pin which we can trade for supplies."

"Supplies! But it was a gift from my mother. Surely it is worth—"

"I'd be grateful if it were worth a pair of horses and enough food."

"But—"

"Elizabeth." His voice lowered in warning.

She studied him in silence, seeing the bruises that had begun to darken his cheekbone, and the blood that was drying on his face. He had done his best to protect her, and it had worked. She could have been the prize to a band of thieves intent on ransom or something far worse.

Suddenly dizzy, she staggered toward the meandering brook they'd followed. She cupped water and brought it to her mouth, then splashed her hot face. She glanced over as John knelt beside her and did the same. When she realized that he was trying to wash away blood, she felt a moment of shame. Should a wife help with such things when there were no physicians about? He had been trying to save her, after all.

"You've missed a spot," she said.

He sat quietly while she dipped the hem of her skirt in the water and dabbed at the blood on the side of his face.

"This will need sewing by a physician," she added.

He shrugged. "It will heal by itself. Then I'll have another scar to show you."

Elizabeth blushed at the memory of his naked body and the fine mapping of scars he'd displayed so proudly, as if it were an honor to be so marked. She suddenly realized how close together they were, that she practically knelt in his lap. She backed away.

Up until this point, she'd managed to keep people between them, except for that one night at the inn. But now they were alone, impoverished, unprotected.

"I don't have any of my healing potions or herbs," she said, wringing her hands together.

"What did you say?" He looked at her with surprise and perhaps even respect.

"Mother said I didn't need them for the journey. I could cleanse your wound with wine, but we don't even have that…" She trailed off.

"Elizabeth."

Panicky, she continued, "If I had marigold, I could make a salve."

Compromised

"Elizabeth, be at peace. I will be well."

~oOo~

To John's relief, it didn't take long to find a farmer more than willing to accept Elizabeth's bauble in exchange for two plain but sturdy horses and a few days worth of supplies. Her court finery, seldom seen so far north, drew plenty of stares as they traveled. And beneath her gown, she still wore that ridiculous farthingale to flare her skirts wide at her waist. She clung to it as her only possession left, even though she had to be so careful on horseback. But she was a decent horsewoman, as he kept reminding himself whenever she exasperated him.

He still was quite amazed at her discussion of how best to heal him. He hadn't thought she'd known of such things, and felt guilty for assuming she was ignorant of such an important wifely skill. Apparently a London-bred earl's daughter knew more than just fashions from France.

That night, he led her off the main road into a clearing in the forest and dismounted, while she remained on her horse. Twilight settled about them in a lush, warm haze as he gazed up into her beautiful face, and for a moment, he thought he was a lucky man.

But then she opened her mouth.

"I cannot stay here," she said, looking down at him wild-eyed. "That village we passed would have been—"

"Stop this, Elizabeth." He shared a long-suffering look with his new horse as pulled off the saddle. "We have no money to pay for lodging. Asking for shelter in the village would only lead to a foul mound of hay in a dilapidated barn. At least now we're under the stars—and alone."

He touched her knee, and she pulled away from him.

81

He laughed. "Allow me to help you down."

"I can—"

Hauling her off the horse, he set her on her feet. She staggered and would have fallen but for his grip on her arms.

"Elizabeth?"

With a pained expression, she limped away from him. "I am merely stiff."

"And now you know why I wanted to help you."

She hesitated, then murmured, "Thank you."

He watched her hobble about the clearing, wondering when she had last ridden a horse for any length of time.

"I'm going into the forest to look for firewood," he said. "I would appreciate your help."

"Firewood?"

He clasped his hands behind his back and spoke with deliberate slowness. "Sticks on the ground."

Even by the setting sun, he could see her blush. "I've never done anything like that."

"There's a first time for everything," he murmured, his gaze dropping down her body.

"I'll stay here," she quickly replied.

Unsurprised that she'd avoid being alone with him every chance she could, John turned and stepped between the trees. He hadn't gone far before he heard her voice.

"Wait! John, wait!"

She caught up with him, her wide skirts scraping between two trees.

"I—I did not wish to be alone," she said, then admitted, "I don't know what sort of wood to look for."

"Then I'll teach you."

Compromised

She soon insisted on carrying some of the wood he found. Though he pointed out it would dirty her sleeves, she rolled her eyes at him as if he was being foolish. And he felt better.

Using the flint and steel from the pouch at his waist, he started a small fire, then spread a blanket for Elizabeth to sit upon. She squinted down at it, uncertainly smoothing her skirts, which hung bell-shaped from her waist.

"You should remove that farthingale," John said. "You don't need it on this journey."

"My father brought it from Spain! I was the first woman in London to wear it. Who knows if I'll ever be able to purchase another one."

"Are you worrying that I might not be able to keep clothing on your back?"

"I know little of your wealth, after all."

"Family and home are more important than money."

"People who don't have money say that," she said tartly. "Exactly what is your worth?"

He strung the bow he'd bartered for that afternoon. "Enough to keep any reasonable person happy."

There was a strained silence between them as she obviously heard the slight against her.

A long moment later, Elizabeth said softly, "What are you doing?"

"Seeing to your food. Unless you'd like to live on biscuits, dried apples, and—"

He saw a movement out of the corner of his eye, turned, and let loose an arrow.

She gave a little squeak of surprise. "Whatever did you do that for?" she demanded.

"Supper."

Elizabeth's growling stomach suffered a twinge of nausea as she watched John pick up the dead rabbit. She was used to seeing her food sumptuously prepared with seasonings and sauces, not dead, fuzzy, and…bloody. When he tossed it at her feet, she jumped back.

"Do you wish to skin it?" he asked wryly.

"I don't know how." She knew her voice had an edge of hysteria to it, and she cursed herself for being a fool. But it was dark, and the wind whistled through the trees, and she was alone with him, and she was so hungry. Suddenly everything seemed overwhelming and miserable.

"No one ever taught me to prepare a simple meal," she added dispiritedly.

"You had servants for that."

It was the truth, but he almost sounded like he was reassuring her, which didn't make sense. She was a failure on this journey, after all.

"If I had married—" She broke off at the cold gleam that suddenly appeared in his eyes as he advanced toward her.

"Well?" he demanded. "Aren't you going to finish explaining what you're thinking?"

He seemed as tall as the trees as she arched her neck to look up at him. She was alone with him—a stranger she'd known mere days, her husband, who now controlled her fate and her very survival.

Chapter 7

Elizabeth took a calming breath and forced her fears into submission, reminding herself that even if she'd married Lord Wyndham, she would have been at his mercy. And what had she known about him? She tried to imagine Lord Wyndham fighting off thieves, bartering for goods, and providing a meal for her, and could not. Still, she'd sent him that letter, had told him there was hope for them. She didn't want to think about that. "I was only going to say was that if I had married anyone else, I would still be in London, with servants."

John shook his head and picked up the dead rabbit. "And you never would have known what new and wonderful things you would be learning."

"Skinning a rabbit?" She shuddered as she saw its blood drip to the ground.

He gave a half-smile, and again his gaze drifted down her body, lingering on her breasts. "I can think of things you will enjoy learning even more. I've showed you some already."

She bit her lip remembering the private and embarrassing things he'd done to her. And how much she'd reveled in it.

"Are you blushing?" he asked softly.

"No." Even his smile made her feel strange inside.

"Come, then, while there's still light. You can watch me prepare roasted rabbit."

Elizabeth forced herself to watch while John skinned the rabbit, but closed her eyes and winced when he cut off the head and gutted the inside. Only when the carcass was mounted on a stick, roasting over the fire did she relax. Soon, the smell coming from it made her stomach begin a chorus of gurgling.

"You may sit down next to me," he said, pointing to a log he'd rolled from the woods, "but you'll have to get rid of that farthingale."

She ignored his request and settled gracefully onto the log, her skirts and farthingale spread around her. She pretended that her gown wasn't dirty and emanating the smell of horse.

John shook his head. "So sitting is one of the skills you've been taught, eh?"

She ignored his teasing. "Do you think…my friend Katherine is looking up at the same stars, as frightened as I am?" When he didn't immediately speak, she added, "No, that's wrong. I'm frightened of the future, and my own ignorance. She could be frightened of something so much worse."

"Don't assume what you don't know. You could be upsetting yourself over your friend for nothing."

"You don't have a very high opinion of women, if you think my dear friend would abandon me on my wedding day, without a word, because of 'nothing.'"

"I didn't mean to make your fears worse."

She made no response, her emotions jumbled. Part of her was so afraid of being alone on a journey with only one man—her husband, yet a stranger. She didn't know Katherine's predicament, which made her feel guilty for being with John, a strong man who was doing his best to take care of her.

"Might I tell you a story to amuse you while we wait for our meal?" he asked.

She glanced at him suspiciously. "What is it about?"

" 'Tis a story of my youth. My brother and I did something very foolish when we were young, and hunting for the first time without our father."

She knew he was trying to distract her, and she reluctantly appreciated it. "What happened?"

He glanced sideways at her, the firelight playing across the strong bones of his face. Maybe he was just as surprised as she was that she wanted to hear the story.

"Oh, we were so young and cocky, I with twelve years, William with nine. We roamed our father's lands and thought we knew everything. We carried our bows, with a quiver of arrows on our backs. We'd each shot rabbits before, under our father's watchful eyes."

"You sound as if you were fond of your father."

As he stared into the fire, he smiled, although his eyes were sad. "Aye, he was a good man. He died about five years ago."

"I am sorry."

"Thank you," he said, the smile reaching his eyes as he studied her.

It was a moment of connection that both surprised and unnerved her. She looked away. "So did you find any more rabbits on your childhood hunting trip?"

"No, and we were frustrated. We followed a trail through the woods, which led to the shallowest ford of a river. But as we came out of the trees, we saw a wolf drinking at the river."

"A wolf? It didn't run off when it saw you?"

"We didn't wait around to see. William turned and ran, and I had to follow him and keep him safe, as the elder brother. Or so I told myself. We thought for certain we heard it following us. I jumped into the lower branches of a tree and pulled William up behind me. We climbed as high as we could, and stayed there—for hours. William pissed—relieved himself—"

As if she hadn't heard the word before.

"—right off the side, and almost fell doing so. We couldn't keep our balance or hold on any longer."

"Where was the wolf?"

"We didn't see it. We hung in the lowest branches before jumping, feeling like our dangling legs were bait, luring a fierce wolf to jump out from the forest. Finally we dropped to the ground and cowered together, but nothing happened."

"He was gone."

"Oh, no, he'd just been waiting for us."

She arched a brow. "You didn't die," she pointed out. "And I saw no signs of scars from a mauling."

"You examined me that closely?" he asked with a smile.

She flushed. "I did not. But such scars would be noticeable. What happened?"

"He came running at us, knocked me over and began to lick my face. He was a shepherd's dog, not a wolf. We'd stayed in the tree for nothing."

She shook her head.

"You didn't laugh."

Compromised

"And why should I laugh? There could be a wolf out there right now." She looked over her shoulder. "I keep thinking I see firelight glittering in an animal's eyes."

He sighed. "I thought to distract you, but I only reminded you of our plight."

"I didn't have to be reminded of something I already knew. But I appreciated the thought. And you seem to be a kind brother."

"I could be a kind husband," he said softly.

She stiffened. "Now that you've schemed to have my dowry?"

"I keep telling you I didn't do that."

She opened her mouth to protest, then let it go. "I don't want to fight."

He nodded. "Neither do I."

They both turned to look into the fire and remained silent.

When the meal was ready, she was so hungry that even the prospect of eating with her fingers didn't dismay her. The meat tasted so good it could have been prepared in the queen's kitchens. Between them, they devoured the entire rabbit.

In the darkness, she sat drowsily before the fire, watching John finish the last of the meat. "Do you think the thieves have followed us?" she asked.

He glanced at her. "Nay. They already took everything we had. Are you still frightened?"

She shook her head quickly, then glanced up as the hoot of an owl echoed through the dark forest. When he put a gentle hand on her arm, she pulled away, troubled by how his consideration made her feel. First he wanted to distract her with stories, and now he thought his touch would soothe her.

And it did, and she didn't know what to think about that.

"I need to clean up," she mumbled, holding her hands out before her.

"Greasy?" he asked.

The laughter in his voice irritated her. How could he be jovial, when they'd lost everything? She took a deep breath to berate him, but he rose and knelt before her. In the darkness his hair and eyes blended mysteriously into the shadows, and she shivered, too fascinated to move.

He took her hands in his and turned them palm up. He placed a kiss in one palm, and a delicious budding of heat uncurled inside her.

And then he licked her, and she gave a little jump and tried to pull away, but he didn't let go. Somehow her voice had deserted her.

He glanced up at her from beneath the fall of his hair. "You taste good," he rumbled in a low murmur, then sucked one of her fingers right into his mouth.

Elizabeth's jaw dropped in shock, and she couldn't seem to swallow, or take a deep enough breath. He must certainly feel the shaking that began in her hands and spread throughout her whole body. He licked and sucked each of her fingers slowly, completely, until she thought she would dissolve from the pleasure of it. There was a hot ache between her thighs that nothing could appease but his touch.

And then she remembered his promise to seduce her. When he pressed her hands against his cheeks, and she felt his warm, stubbled skin, she knew this had to stop. Pulling away, she stood up, forcing him to sit back on his heels.

He gave her a bemused smile. "Is something wrong?"

"I'm going to wash in the stream," she said, hating the unfamiliar choked sound of her voice.

"Elizabeth, you shouldn't wander off by yourself," he called, then chuckled as she practically ran from him. "Watch out for dogs!"

Away from the fire it was dark and cooler. She slowed to let her eyes adjust to the shadows of the uneven ground and the sloping bank of the river. As the sound of gurgling water drew her, she fell to her knees and plunged her aching hands in, as if she could scrub away the memory of his mouth on her skin.

She sat back on her heels and looked out at the rippling water, with the moon reflecting off it and dancing in her eyes. She was afraid of John, afraid of what she felt, more than she was afraid of the wild forest. Every moment of her life with him was filled with things she didn't know how to do, new ways to disappoint him and herself.

If only she had the courage to triumph in this intimate battle between them. Maybe she could prove to herself that she had control of at least a small portion of her life.

When she looked over her shoulder, he was sprawled leisurely on the far side of the fire, propping his head on one arm, watching her. She climbed up the bank of the stream, marched to her side of the fire, and glared at the hard ground.

"It's more comfortable over here," he called in a deep, soft voice.

Defiantly holding his gaze, she reached up beneath her skirt and untied her farthingale, then stepped out and set it aside.

He grinned. "Warmer, too."

"As if I need that on this night," she said. "I'll be writing a letter home to my father. If you're thinking to prove yourself worthy of my dowry, I'm sure this will not help your cause."

He continued to smile, as if her hollow threat amused him. "The fact that I saved your life will be looked on poorly by your father?"

She lay down on her back and looked up at the sky, lit with pinpricks of light. "Nay, just the fact that you're forcing me to travel under such circumstances."

" 'Tis a shame that no one saw fit before now to teach you to withstand life's problems with more grace."

She bit her lip and felt a rush of tears sting her eyes. Rolling onto her side, she faced away from the fire, away from her husband.

~oOo~

It had taken John a long time to fall asleep, and he had hoped that somehow a new day would make things miraculously better. Instead at dawn a heavy rain began. He shook Elizabeth awake. Sitting up with weariness, she watched him saddle the horses, while water dripped through her hair.

"Is there anything to eat?" she asked.

"Dried apples and cheese in the saddle bag."

She heaved a sigh. "When will we be there?"

He patted the horse's neck absently, in his mind seeing not the animal's brown coat, but his estate and the centuries-old castle that dominated the land for miles in every direction, still several days distant. He could almost see the two of them arriving miserable with each other. Just the thought of his brother's sympathy and his mother's disappointment was enough to set his teeth on edge. How could he explain that his foolish inability to control himself around Elizabeth had resulted in such a marriage?

But by evening he and Elizabeth would be able to reach his hunting lodge, and a respite there would give John a chance to think and prepare.

The rain had not let up by nightfall, and if anything, the humidity seemed worse. When he steered the horses off the road and onto a small wooded path, Elizabeth finally broke her weary silence.

"What is this? Where are we going?" Her face was pale and dripped with rain, her hair tumbled in muddy disarray down her back.

"Our home."

Before he could explain that it was only one of his homes, a hunting lodge, he watched her face go ashen, and she actually seemed to brace herself as if preparing for squalor. He bit back any explanations and waited for the rest of her reaction.

In the gloom of approaching night, the small stone and timber lodge looked forlorn, abandoned. John glanced at Elizabeth, whose wide eyes stared about her.

"Is there…a village?" she asked.

He shook his head.

"Neighbors?" Her voice grew even weaker.

"If there were, I'm sure not the kind you're used to."

"But—you're a baron. Doesn't living like this bother you?"

93

"No." Part of him felt guilty for misleading her, but here he could have one last chance to know and understand her. It would be a test, a way to be certain she could really be his wife—in every way—without the prying eyes of his family and his servants, without her seeing his castle and holdings and thinking she'd gotten everything she wanted.

She bit her lip, then murmured, "Well, shall we get out of the rain?"

They left the horses to graze while they entered the lodge. John watched Elizabeth closely as she took in the dust, gloom, and shadows. There was a table and benches, two chairs before the hearth, cupboards and trunks, and a bed in the corner. He saw her swallow.

"Is this—the only chamber?" she asked.

He nodded. "Let me open the shutters so you can see it by the last of the day's light."

But although the gloom lifted as he threw back the shutters from four windows, the light only showed how much dust had accumulated since he'd been there last spring.

"I'll make a fire before I put the horses in the barn."

"Must you? It's so hot."

"We need to heat water and cook food, do we not?" he asked gently.

"Oh, of course. I tried to watch you make a fire while we traveled, but it was difficult. I'll pay more attention."

He blinked at her in surprise. "Why?" he asked, trying to hide his skepticism.

"Because the fire might go out when you're not here."

"Then we'll have to huddle together for warmth when I get back."

94

Compromised

She remained serious, ignoring his teasing. "I'd prefer to be more knowledgeable, regardless." She hesitated. "I'm not skilled at learning new things."

He straightened and studied her, reminded that Nicholas had said their parents stressed her beauty as if it was all she had. Yet here she was, trying to learn something new, even though she was obviously miserable. Every day there seemed to be something new to admire in his wife as she adjusted to a different world than she'd grown up in. She didn't hold him back; she pushed herself to be his equal as they traveled. She didn't complain much about their long days on poor roads, although she did challenge him with questions. She was a strong, beautiful woman, but didn't seem to give herself credit for it—although much of her problems with self-worth were because of her parents. If only she could be eager to see what their future was, instead of dreading it.

Elizabeth tried hard to concentrate on what John showed her, but she found her gaze roaming the tiny room, smaller than her bedchamber in her father's manor. She was stunned that John thought nothing of the two of them living forever in close quarters, with only each other for company.

But after a day of awkward silence between them, she was relieved that he was smiling at her again. Without his good nature, everything seemed duller, more miserable, and she felt discouraged with herself that she already relied on his even temper and gentle humor.

When John suddenly stood up, she took a quick step backward.

" 'Tis time to remove those wet clothes," he said.

His voice deepened, roughened, and she closed her eyes, wondering when she would get used to its effect on her. There was a timbre in his voice that took her back to mornings in bed, pressed against his warm skin, his knowledgeable hands bringing her body to life. She wanted to protest removing her garments, but knew he was right. He unlaced her gown at the back. She could have done it herself, but wet laces made things difficult. After he began to push it down over her shoulders, she clutched it against her chest and stepped away from him.

"I can finish this myself. Thank you." She shivered at the dampness.

"Wait." He caught her by the hips and pulled her back. "Your skin is rubbed raw right here."

He touched the skin just below her shoulder, where the seams of her garments met and shrank with the rain. Though there was a tiny sting, that was nothing next to the feel of his hands on her, the way he rubbed her bare shoulders.

"Oh, Elizabeth," he murmured.

She felt his breath on her neck only a moment before he pressed his mouth there. He said her name over and over, parting her garments down her back, dropping to his knees to kiss everything he laid bare to her waist.

She swayed with numbing weakness, longing to fall into his arms and let him carry her to bed. She would be warm, protected, loved—

Her thoughts came to a reeling halt and she pulled away from him. He did not love her.

Over her shoulder, she saw John rest his hand on the floor as if bracing himself, his head bent. Then with a sigh he arose.

Compromised

"I'll see to the horses," he said. "In one of the trunks there should be shirts, doublets, and hose, but no female garments. I'll bring you water from the well, so you can wash yourself."

As he left, she groaned and covered her face with her hands. What had she been thinking? Of course he didn't love her! He loved her money, and only tried to seduce her so she wouldn't tell her father all that had befallen her, so he'd be certain to earn that dowry after the year he'd mentioned to trick her father. He'd brought her to this dank, tiny cottage, where he'd expect her money to improve their lives, not his own hard work.

But the words she'd been using to try to convince herself rang hollow. He'd protected her, defended her, and treated her gently. As poor Katherine had said, every nobleman expected a dowry.

She had a sudden image of sitting beside John at this table, with laughing children surrounding them.

Elizabeth groaned again. What was happening to her, that being part of a family with John no longer frightened her?

Chapter 8

After John set water to heat over the fire, he found musty, but dry, linens for Elizabeth to wash with. He thought she almost asked if there was a tub, but caught herself in time. It was still a great regret of his that he hadn't been able to watch her skin glisten with water at the inn, watch her soap her slim legs or take down her hair. He would have cherished such a memory forever. Instead he'd remain in the corridor, head near the door, listening, imagining. He would see such a sight someday, he told himself. It would take patient wooing on his behalf, but he was determined to try. But could he convince Elizabeth to meet him halfway? He wanted to keep her all to himself. Maybe…somehow she could come to accept their marriage, to love him.

He took his time in the barn, giving her the privacy he knew she wanted. But it was physically painful not to be there when she removed her garments, when she stood naked before the fire. His mind went back to imagining the wet cloth sliding over her skin, leaving her glistening in the flickering light.

He shook his head, cursing himself for a romantic fool.

When he returned to the lodge, he found Elizabeth seated before the fire, one of his shirts dwarfing her, his hose drooping down her legs. He should be amused that she thought the hose necessary for bed, but instead found himself admiring the long, blond hair tumbling down to her waist. Even garbed so, she managed to look incredibly feminine, delicate and appealing.

She put her hands on her hips. "I feel ridiculous. When my gown is dry, I'll put it back on."

"You don't look ridiculous," he said hoarsely.

"I cannot be the wife of a baron and look like this. I had such plans for my wardrobe."

"I didn't think you'd need all those London garments."

"It's not about that. I didn't want to be beholden to you."

He blinked. "But I'm your husband."

"And it is up to the wife to oversee her household. There is money in fabric, can you not see that?"

He was speechless.

"I spent hours of the early part of our journey planning how I would repurpose the fabric from gowns I wouldn't wear, how I would cut them up for linens and draperies or plainer gowns. I had perfectly calculated the money I would save."

Calculated? She'd made plans for how best to spend her money?

"And then they were all stolen," she finished, crossing her arms over her chest and frowning.

"I will make certain you have all the fabric you need for such…calculations."

She didn't react to his teasing.

"I never thought I'd see the day a woman looked good in men's garb, but you shine in whatever you wear, Elizabeth."

She turned away, blushing.

But he was wrong about the reason, because she turned back and faced him angrily, her face blotchy red. "Stop complimenting me when it's not true. It feels like you're trying to manipulate me, as if you think I'm so ignorant"—she drew in a shaky breath—"that I'll become suddenly pliable to your wishes because of some pretty words that are really lies."

He straightened his shoulders and faced her soberly. "We don't know each other well, even after days of constant togetherness. But Elizabeth, I don't lie. I haven't lied once to you, not during our marriage negotiations, not during our journey. And I'm getting tired of your constant slurs on my character. I think you're beautiful, and it doesn't matter if you're soaked in rain, covered in mud, or perspiring from a hot day."

He felt a twinge of guilt, knowing he wasn't lying about the hunting lodge, but he was leaving out certain facts.

Her mouth sagged open and her skin went pale, but he took no mercy on her.

He pointed a finger at her. "Perhaps you need to look inside yourself and wonder why you're so quick to believe that you can't be attractive when you're not dressed in your London finery. Beauty isn't just your face, but everything inside you that shines from your eyes, from your expressions, from your heart. You don't believe in yourself, Elizabeth, and it's a damn shame."

He wanted her to defend herself, to fight back, to *believe* in herself. But she pressed her lips together, eyes narrowed, and said nothing.

"What is this about calculations you make in your head?" he demanded.

"It is about numbers," she said stiffly.

Compromised

"I don't make swift calculations in my head—most people don't. That's a skill you can be proud of, but instead you're defensive, as if it doesn't matter." He shook his head and changed the subject. "I'll make supper. We keep dry stores here."

He expected her to be so angry at him that she avoided him, but instead she stood beside him stiffly and studied what he did. She didn't ask questions, so he started explaining everything as he went. He thought she tried hard to pay attention, but occasionally he saw her gazing about the room, her eyes wide and overwhelmed. Every time she saw him studying her, she glared at him. Another thing he could say about his new wife—she didn't back down from a challenge. After being robbed, many people would have given up.

He boiled dried peas and beans into a watery soup, and made oatcakes. She eyed the food curiously when she took a bowl full, but he'd added several spices like salt and dried parsley, and she nodded in surprise after taking a spoonful.

He didn't expect her to be talkative after their argument, but the silence was awkward, and he knew she had to be imagining endless meals alone in the cottage with him for the rest of her life.

"You could tell me my flaws, you know," he said at last.

She eyed him. "I beg your pardon?"

"Marriage should be about listening to each other."

"You think you know everything about marriage," she said dryly.

"Aren't any of your brothers married?"

"No. But yours is, and they have so many children, they must have the *perfect* marriage."

He felt a little uncomfortable, because it certainly seemed that way to him, but he refrained from saying so. "Nothing is perfect. Go ahead, tell me my flaws. Surely you want to."

"Very well." She looked down her beautiful nose at him. "You are a man who expects perfection."

He stiffened in outrage. "I do not. You wanted to watch me cook and learn from it—I didn't expect you to know how to do it."

She rolled her eyes. "This isn't about cooking, but marriage. Why were no Yorkshire women good enough to be your wife?"

"Because I didn't meet anyone who suited me."

"In what way? You've already claimed beauty is not all you care about."

"I want to be able to have conversations with my wife, to laugh with good humor, to rear our children in tranquility, to see the world in the same way. And don't say anything about dowries, or this conversation is done."

She arched a brow. "I didn't. But I still feel you are expecting, if not perfection, than a perfect match. No woman is perfect."

"So I was supposed to settle for some woman I didn't feel was the right wife for me?"

"That would have been better for both of us, would it not?"

"We cannot change the past, Elizabeth. What's done is done."

"You asked me to tell you one of your flaws, and I did. There's no need to be defensive."

Compromised

She was trying to turn his words back on him. It was his turn to roll his eyes. "I'm going to close up the barn for the night."

When he returned, he found Elizabeth already in bed, the blankets pulled up to her neck as she faced the wall. Even in this unbearable heat, she felt the need to cover herself from his gaze. But he knew the truth—she was covering herself as if to guard against how he could make her feel. She might be cool to marriage, but she erupted into flames when he touched her. He stood over her, watching her breathe slowly, evenly—in too-perfect rhythm.

He heaved a great sigh and murmured as if he believed her asleep, "Well, I hope she thought to shake the bugs out of the bedding."

She flung back the blankets and launched herself out of the bed. Laughing, he caught her against him. She was so unpredictable, his Elizabeth. She'd surprised him by trying hard to follow his example with chores, then reacted exactly as he expected about insects. He would never be bored in this marriage.

When she sputtered her outrage, he couldn't help kissing her, holding her soft body against his, slanting his open mouth across hers.

When she turned her head away, John groaned with frustration. "Why did you stop? You liked that, Elizabeth, I know you did."

"Don't think you can make me jump out of the bed only to lie back on it with you. I told you I won't be forced."

"Elizabeth," he whispered, pressing kisses to her cheek. "How much longer do you think I can wait? I want to caress you, to make you wet for me—"

"Stop!" She bowed her head. "I—I cannot trust you."

He let her go and she stumbled back.

"I don't even know how we'll survive," she added solemnly. "How can you feed us here in the depths of the forest without fields to plant?"

"I can take care of you," he insisted, regretting the facts he'd kept hidden. But if she knew he was wealthy, he could never be certain her loyalty was to him—or to his money. "Why can you not trust me? Do you think I would let my wife starve, or go about garbed in sackcloth?"

"I'm already garbed in your clothing. For a lady, there's not much difference. You cannot do anything without my dowry, and we won't have that for at least a year, if ever. I don't even know how to live this sort of life." She waved a listless hand about the room. Then her sorrowful eyes met his. "What if I disappoint you by being unable to learn?"

She feared not being able to please him? That was a very good sign.

"I won't be disappointed as long as you try," he answered, surprised at how hoarse his voice sounded. "You'll have me as husband, Elizabeth. I still have hopes that that will be enough."

She closed her eyes and turned away, murmuring, "I'm worried you've set your hopes too high, John."

She began to strip the bed. When the sheets and blankets were draped over her arms, she finally looked up at him with tired eyes. "Where should I shake these out? I don't want to trail them in the dirt."

Compromised

While he helped her outside, he cursed himself for the foolish emotions which made him ache for her acceptance. Could he be falling in love with her? God help him, for she could crush his heart.

~oOo~

When John awoke with Elizabeth warm and soft in his arms, he told himself the day would go well, that she would adjust to their marriage, that he would be able to take her home to his family soon. In sleep, her expression was untroubled, her skin luminous in the dusky gray of early morning that filtered in through the shutters. He thought about awakening her as he had at the inn, but there was only so much a man could take. He didn't want to lose control and seduce her out of her virginity, when he'd vowed he would wait for her to accept him.

But she lifted her head off his chest, and looked up through strands of her hair at him. Her eyes suddenly widened with realization, and for a long moment they simply looked at each other. He imagined her kissing him, rising up to straddle his hips—but instead she slipped out of bed. Though her gown was still damp and filthy, she dressed in it, even putting that cursed farthingale back on, as if to remind him of the life he'd taken her from.

Or to remind herself? Was she trying to cling to this symbol of her past because she was being drawn into a new future? Could he slowly but surely be wearing her resistance down?

The day's chores didn't help.

"What are we doing first?" she asked, hands on her hips as she regarded him.

"'We'?" he echoed.

105

"Did you think I would sit here and do nothing?"

"I plan to have a servant or two."

"But until then, there is too much work for one person. I can learn."

She sounded like she was convincing herself more than him, but that was fine.

"We'll need more firewood," he said.

She pivoted toward the door and went outside. He stood in the doorway and watched her march along the trees and begin to pick up sticks and small logs, holding them in her skirts. He searched the other side of the clearing, but had a hard time watching what he was doing, when he could be watching her. Since he wasn't paying attention, he ended up dropping a log on his foot, and Elizabeth saw the whole thing. She only shook her head and moved slowly toward the hunting lodge, her skirts straining with their load.

Limping, John got to the doorway in time to see her dump everything she held onto the fire. Ashes shot outward and coated her face. It took everything in him not to laugh, especially when she turned to gape at him, her eyes and teeth the only white part left of her face. He said nothing, only knelt to stack his bundle to the side of the hearth.

"I thought I'd save time," she said faintly.

"'Twas a good effort. Now let me clean you off."

He dipped a rag in a basin of water and she stood quietly before him as he began to wipe her face. It streaked more than disappeared, and he was starting to wonder if she'd need full immersion in water to rid herself of it.

She was studying him too quietly, too thoughtfully.

"What are you thinking?" he asked.

106

Compromised

"You could have berated my foolishness."

"Why would I do that? You're trying to help."

She looked away from him, biting her lip. He imagined her parents had dismissed everything she'd tried to do. How would he have felt, growing up believing himself useless except for the prominent marriage one could bring the family? And yet here she was, making the best of things. She had a strength deep inside no one had ever encouraged her to draw on.

Then she coughed. "Ashes taste awful."

Smiling, he said nothing, only continued to wipe her face. The wood she'd added caught fire, the flames rose higher, but he didn't pay much attention to it—until the odor changed.

Elizabeth frowned. "Is it getting hotter?"

And then she dove toward him, and he caught her, dragging her away from the hearth. Her hemline was on fire, and he grabbed a bucket of water to douse it. She'd dropped to her knees to beat the flames.

"Are you burned?" he asked, searching her face.

She shook her head, wide-eyed, before her shoulders started to shake.

"Don't cry. What can I do?"

She fell back on the floor, the farthingale rounding her skirts toward the timbered ceiling. And then he realized she was laughing, that her smudged face couldn't hide the beauty of her full smile, a sight he'd never seen before. He sat back on his heels and just stared at her in wonder.

She briefly covered her face as if she could wipe her smirk away, but it didn't work. She met his gaze helplessly.

"So…sorry. I don't know why this seems funny. What else could possibly go wrong?"

"Don't say that."

"You're right, of course." She tried to alter her expression into seriousness, but her dancing eyes betrayed her.

As they stared at each other, their smiles slowly faded. She was lying there on the floor, and all he had to do was lean over to kiss her.

As if she realized the same thing, she scrambled to her feet, pushing her farthingale down. "I'll…fill the bucket from the well." She walked quickly outside.

Chapter 9

As Elizabeth pulled the bucket up from the depth of the well, her mind raced over what she'd just experienced with John. After their tense conversation the night before, when she'd told him he expected perfection, and he'd insisted that wasn't true, she'd been determined to do her part. She was still mortified that she'd confessed her fears that she'd disappoint him by being unable to learn. That was something she'd only considered in her own mind; she'd never shared it with anyone else, not even Katherine. It was humiliating to confess one's secret thoughts. But he already knew she didn't believe in herself; it was apparent to even a man who barely knew her.

But he'd tried to convince her that sincere effort was what mattered, not the outcome. He didn't seem to think her unnatural because she did sums in her head. And then she'd answered that with cynicism. Somewhere in the night she'd been ashamed of herself, and had determined to ignore her own worst instincts. John seemed to think better of her—surely she could feel the same way.

But she'd made a mess of things, figuratively and literally. The simplest things seemed difficult to her, like collecting wood and managing not to get burned. Of course the farthingale didn't help matters where the fire was concerned. Why did she keep wearing it? Wasn't she being rather silly?

But everything of her past had been stolen or sold. She felt adrift in this new life, with John her only anchor. And it was frightening.

She'd give up the farthingale, but not yet. She wasn't quite ready for him to say "I told you so," not that he'd actually say that, she thought sourly. He sometimes seemed too good to be true, a man offended at her slurs against his honor where her dowry was concerned, a man who supported her and defended her—and desired her.

She shivered, remembering waking up, again, in his arms. How much longer would he let her make the decisions about their marriage bed? Just another way the man was noble and kind. Wincing at her own flaws, she carried the bucket inside, only to find John strapping a quiver of arrows to his back, a bow on the table.

"I'm going to hunt some meat for dinner," he said. "Will you be well here alone?"

Alone. When had she ever been alone in her life? There'd always been family and servants and her friends in the busy town of London.

But she'd promised herself she'd make more of an effort. "I'll be fine."

He nodded, and if he had his doubts, she appreciated that he didn't say so. Damn, how was she supposed to live up to someone who was always so perfect? Of course he expected perfection in others—he was always striving for that state himself!

"If you want to keep busy," he continued, "there's a vegetable garden outside. See if there's something to harvest for our meal. There'll be plenty of weeds to comb through. You could take care of those, too."

Compromised

"Very well," she said, when she wanted to say that the only times she'd been in a vegetable was to pass through on the way to the lady's garden, which was filled with flowers that only satisfied the eye and the nose, not the stomach.

After he left, she stood in the open doorway, watching until he disappeared into the shadows of the trees. It sounded…quiet, too quiet. Somewhere in the distance birds sang to each other, but they stopped, and then there was nothing.

She told herself that the birds were in fear of John, not dangerous beasts or murdering villains. But she closed the door and leaned against it, looking around the small room as if it were her sanctuary.

My, how her thoughts had changed in just twenty-four hours.

But no, she was trying to prove herself today. She'd look for vegetables, as John requested. But she took a knife with her, too, to defend herself—and to cut vegetables. Did one cut them, or pull them? She'd heard the servants talk about pulling weeds, but not pulling vegetables. Well, she'd find out.

The moment she left the shade of the cottage, the sun beat down on her hair. Without a veil for protection, she'd suffer, but it couldn't be helped. She tied her hair back with a piece of leather, hoping it would at least protect her neck. She circled the cottage, to the dilapidated barn, with its little paddock where their horses grazed. She went to pet their noses and make sure they had water in their trough. They almost felt like companions.

And then she couldn't avoid her chores any longer. There was a broad section of ground with a woven fence around it. But the greenery within seemed scattered and haphazard, not the neat rows she remembered in the gardens tended by her servants. But of course, John had been absent for several weeks. If he'd paid people to tend the garden, they hadn't done competent work. It would be up to her to oversee it now. Perhaps she should start with pulling the weeds. She took a moment to remove the farthingale and set it aside. Plenty of time to put it back on before John returned.

After a couple hours, her fingernails were broken, her hands dirty and sore, but she felt pleased with herself. She could see a few neat rows now, even though she'd done less than a quarter of the garden. She wasn't certain what vegetables made up each row, but that would come next.

"Elizabeth?"

She gave a start, having not even heard him approach. And she hadn't put her farthingale back on. She rose stiffly to her knees and turned to see him holding a line where several dead birds were tied. She grimaced, but she was getting used to the sight, considering that she needed to eat.

John frowned with confusion. "Where are the carrots?"

"Carrots?" she echoed.

"See the board at the end of the row, etched with the image of a carrot? There's nothing in the row. I think you removed the greens."

"They weren't weeds?" she said weakly. All that work…

For a moment, he eyed her thoughtfully, as if he might speak. Instead, he bent to dig his fingers into the earth she'd just cleared, and pulled up a dirty carrot, grinning at her. "No harm done. Pick a few more to cook with our meal."

Compromised

Hands on her hips, she scowled at the garden as he walked away, whistling tunelessly. She felt like a fool, and he'd taken her behavior in stride. She didn't know if she felt more relieved or irritated. But she picked a few more carrots and followed him inside.

He set the birds on the table and eyed her. "Would you like to rest? It's been a long day."

"John, it's just past midday. Thank you for your consideration, but I am fine. You're the one who traipsed through the woods looking for game. I will roast the birds."

He didn't even appear to doubt her abilities, just gave her advice and didn't laugh when she overcooked them. She sucked on her scorched finger and eyed the darkened meat with scorn. She'd wanted to prove to herself that she could try hard and do her part, but she felt like a liability, as if she could never be as good a wife as his sister by marriage. When John went out to put the horses in the barn, her frustrations with herself turned into tears that she couldn't control.

When he returned, she was still wiping the tears from her face.

"Elizabeth, are you well?"

She lifted a hand, but didn't turn to face him.

"This is all my fault," he said quietly, his voice full of tired sorrow. "I kept thinking you would adapt, become used to being my wife, but I've only made you miserable. This afternoon, when you made the mistake weeding, but didn't seem very upset by it, I thought things might still turn out well."

She faced him. "John, I'm not crying because of you."

"Do not try to make me feel better."

"John—"

"I can't feel better, because I've been lying to you."

She frowned, studying the desolation in his eyes. "What are you saying?"

"This isn't my home—it's only a hunting lodge. I've never lived here, and you won't have to live here either."

She sucked in a breath, shocked. With every word, she kept expecting to feel relieved, but all that rose within her was anger.

"I have many properties," he continued, "including a castle where my family is in residence right now."

"Why did you lie to me?" Her voice was soft, because if she raised it, she might explode. She'd been thinking him so noble and good, had gotten past her anger about the dowry, had been considering herself so much less than him—and he'd lied to her?

He leaned back against the table and rubbed a hand on his neck. "I hadn't planned it, even told myself it wasn't really a lie, that I was just withholding all the facts. But I saw your face when you thought this was where you'd live forever. And I had a wild feeling that if you would be fine living here, then I'd know we could have a true marriage."

"Like a test," she said coldly.

"Aye, like a test. It was beneath me, and you deserved better."

Her anger made her chest feel hot, made her words come out between gritted teeth. "And that's the terrible part—I thought I *didn't* deserve better. Every day I thought you were more and more above me."

"Elizabeth—"

Compromised

"But I'd been trying my hardest, and you'd been lying. I wanted to make you proud, I wanted you to admire me. But that made me no more than a piece of jewelry, a pretty object to look upon from afar. I'd been treated like that my whole life, and I finally wanted more. I tried to be your wife, your partner, ready to share the joys and sorrows of life." The tears slipped down her cheeks and she didn't bother to dash them away. "I tried to change for you, but you weren't willing to do the same. You couldn't trust in me. The only things men wanted of me—my beauty and my dowry—they're yours now. I hope they're enough."

She got shakily to her feet, glancing at John's sad, regretful expression before she crawled into bed. She fell into an exhausted sleep and never knew if he joined her.

~oOo~

In the morning, Elizabeth awoke without the warm comfort of John within her arms—and then was angry with herself for missing it, missing him. She lifted her head and looked about, though she'd already guessed she was alone. After donning her filthy gown, she half-heartedly ate the berries John had left on the table. She felt exhausted, as if even sleep had not healed the weight of despair she now carried within her. What was she to do or say when he came back through the door? Were they supposed to pretend nothing had happened? She could never do that; he'd tricked her, lied to her, betrayed her.

After an hour of pacing, she heard the jingle of many horses coming near, and the shouts of men. Fear stabbed her belly, and she hugged herself. She was alone, without any defense. Could the thieves have tracked them down?

115

She couldn't just wait and wonder, so she stepped to the window and peered out. There were least a score of soldiers and servants, and in the lead was Lord Wyndham. Relief made her shudder, her shoulders sagging. He was dressed in court finery that glittered out of place in the cool green of the forest. His narrow, handsome face and blond hair usually made her sigh with delight. But something lodged in her throat when she saw John with the traveling party. She opened the door and stood in plain view, chin lifted defiantly.

Her eyes began to sting when Lord Wyndham dismounted and the two men talked. She had forgotten all about the letter she had sent Wyndham, telling him she wasn't happy with her marriage and hinting that she would welcome his attention after an annulment. As John glanced at her, expressionless, she knew he was learning of it.

She realized it was just as much of a betrayal as she'd accused him of last night.

The two men approached the cottage, and Elizabeth saw Wyndham's surprised gaze sweep down her body. She hadn't bothered with her farthingale, so her dirty skirts trailed on the floor; her hair and face hadn't been properly washed. She felt miserable about what she and John had done to each other and their marriage with their lies and mistrust. But worse was John's calm stare. Why wasn't he angry? Why wasn't he drawing her aside to point out how she'd betrayed *him*?

"Elizabeth," John said, "Lord Wyndham received a letter from you on our departure from London, which made him decide to follow us. The villagers in these parts know me and it was easy enough for him to do."

116

Compromised

Of course they knew him, she thought sarcastically—he was a baron with castles and a hunting lodge. But how could she remain bitter when John's voice only seemed tired to her? What could she say?

"He says you would rather come with him than remain married to me."

She opened her mouth, but John held up a hand.

"We both know it's true." His voice softened. "I want nothing more than your happiness, and I know you cannot find it with me."

"Lady Elizabeth," Lord Wyndham began, sweeping into a deep bow, "I wish to marry you."

These were the words she'd always wanted to hear. She'd selfishly schemed to make them happen, only to end up compromising herself and changing her life forever. *Now* Lord Wyndham wanted her. Then why couldn't she keep her eyes off John's face?

Lord Wyndham said, "Lord Malory assures me that your marriage has remained in name only. In fact, he has been so kind as to offer witnesses, your hired servants, who can verify such a thing."

John met her gaze for only a moment before looking away. Was he deliberately sending her away because of her betrayal, or giving her what he assumed she wanted after *his* betrayal? Their entire marriage was such a mess.

"I won't contest an annulment," John said shortly. "Go on, Elizabeth, there's nothing here for you."

She stiffened, then said "Thank you."

When Wyndham took her arm and drew her away from the hunting lodge, she glanced over her shoulder as John went inside and shut the door. The sound of it startled her and she shook, but Lord Wyndham was there, helping her onto a horse, putting her into the care of maidservants. She didn't look back as they led her away.

~oOo~

John knew that it was time to leave the hunting lodge. He should go home, tell his family that he had failed to find a suitable wife, that he would have to try again.

But he couldn't imagine wanting a wife who wasn't Elizabeth.

He spent the day chopping wood to replace the stores they'd used since they arrived. With every stroke of the ax, he tried to make himself believe that he'd done the right thing letting her go. She'd been correct about him—he hadn't trusted her, had lied to her. And she'd told another man she wanted out of their marriage. The difference was, she'd written that letter before they'd spent time together, whereas he'd betrayed her after days of intimacy.

And he couldn't forget how her parents had taught her to devalue herself, to believe she was worth nothing more than the sum of her allowance—no wonder she liked numbers.

Elizabeth thought she could succeed at nothing else besides being beautiful. And then he'd played the fool more than once and compared her to his sister by marriage. God above, all he'd done was confirm in her eyes that she was only a beautiful woman, with little else to offer a man. It made him sick inside to know that maybe he was like her parents after all.

As night descended, he stood alone before the hearth, hearing only the distant animals in the forest, feeling a loneliness he'd never imagined before. Being with Elizabeth had filled an emptiness inside him. He'd watched her grow and change, and had felt the same thing happening to him. For he hadn't just wanted to lie with her—he realized he wanted to earn her love.

He'd given her up to Wyndham too easily.

John smacked his fist against the mantel. He could still see her face when she'd seen Wyndham, the look of wariness and guilt rather than happiness. Without asking her to make a choice, John had given her away like a necklace he no longer wanted.

He had to find her. He had to explain that he was doing what he thought *she* wanted, not what *he* wanted, which was to love her until she finally understood that there were no conditions, that he could change as much as she could.

Morning would be too late. He packed the few supplies he needed—including the farthingale—saddled one of the horses, and set off by moonlight, knowing he had to win Elizabeth back.

Chapter 10

Elizabeth awoke in luxurious surroundings, in the best chamber at the inn, with maidservants sleeping on pallets at her feet. But although she was clean and comfortable for the first time in days, the sick feeling with which she'd gone to bed had not left her.

During their slow journey south yesterday, as a cold rainstorm settled about them, she'd tried to tell herself that leaving John was for the best, that they would never trust each other, could never forget the betrayals. But maybe the truth was, she thought she could never make him happy. She'd been trying, and failing.

But traveling at Lord Wyndham's side had been a revelation. Now that she knew John, she felt as if she were seeing Wyndham with clear eyes for the first time. The man she'd so worshipped back in London treated his servants disdainfully, thoughtlessly, and had talked to the innkeeper in an arrogant manner.

John was courteous even when he was angry with her, and he treated everyone down to the stable boys in a fair manner. He didn't care how she looked; he enjoyed her beauty, but it wasn't important to him. Society's notion of fashionable ladies' attire didn't concern him as much as her comfort.

She remembered his sweet words of encouragement when she'd done nothing but fail at every task. Lord Wyndham hadn't cared that their party had been attacked and how it affected her; he'd simply needed her to bathe and dress quickly, so she wouldn't embarrass him.

But the worst punishment was trying to forget this yearning John had awakened inside her, that made even his nearness more exciting than any other man's touch. Waking up without him, without the possibility of seeing him, had made loneliness ache inside her.

Could she have fallen in love with him?

She felt a prick of tears behind her eyelids as she thought of his gentle humor and kindness. If she went back to him, could they put their mutual mistakes behind them and begin their marriage again? Could he grow to love her even if she wasn't like his sister by marriage?

Elizabeth drew on the reserve of strength she'd only recently discovered within herself. She had to return to John. She had risked everything once, going out to that garden with him; she owed it to both of them to risk it all again.

After the maids helped her dress in the new gown Lord Wyndham had brought for her, Elizabeth joined him in the inn's private dining parlor. He glanced up at her with a nod, but concentrated on his food. She couldn't help but compare him to John, who would have risen to his feet with a frank smile, and made her feel wanted.

When she didn't sit down immediately, Wyndham looked up again. "We're leaving soon, Lady Elizabeth. Do eat something."

"Lord Wyndham, I need to speak with you."

He nodded and continued eating.

She took a deep breath. "I have made a mistake. In all good conscience, I cannot marry you."

121

Wyndham slowly set his knife down and sat back. "The annulment will not be a problem. And I'm certain my family can be persuaded to accept you."

She felt a chill at just the thought. "But my lord, I am married, and I do not wish to end it. I miss my husband."

He regarded her with narrowed eyes. "You miss that uncivilized country lord?"

"He and I suit one another, Lord Wyndham," she said firmly. "With your permission, I would like an escort back to his hunting lodge."

After giving her a dismissive look, he went back to his food. "I think not, Lady Elizabeth. I went through much time and effort because of that ridiculous letter you wrote me. I cannot spare anyone now. And please give that gown back to the maidservants."

She blinked in amazement, and anger heated her words. "Are you saying you wish me to travel alone? In that ragged garment? That you begrudge me even one servant?"

"I am." Though he didn't look up, he smiled.

"But I have calculated the cost of these garments, a horse, and travel supplies. When I return north, I will gladly repay you."

"No."

She shook her head regretfully. "I'm sorry that I played with your affections when I wrote that letter, but I have learned much about myself since then. I can do anything I set my mind to—even traveling alone. Farewell, my lord."

~oOo~

Elizabeth rode the horse she'd stolen from Lord Wyndham along the road that would take her to John's hunting lodge. She was almost certain she would be able to find the wooded path once she came upon it.

122

Compromised

The trees closed in around her as the village grew smaller and smaller behind her. She knew she had many hours of travel yet to go, and she was alone, easy prey for thieves who could be hiding behind any hedge at the side of the road. She kept touching the knife she'd slid into the sheath of her saddle, looking all around her as she rode. Traveling this way was a foolish, dangerous thing to do, but she was beyond caring. She was so afraid John might have left the hunting lodge to go looking for a new wife.

In the distance, she saw another traveler approaching her from the north. She was just entering the forest, and felt small and vulnerable next to the towering trees—and the approaching stranger.

Surely he would ignore her. She looked like she was wearing a noblewoman's old cast-offs. She bowed her head, tried to slump in the saddle, anything to appear old and tired and worn by work.

When she could hear the muffled sound of the other horse's hooves striking dirt, she risked a glance from under her eyebrows. The man was still far enough away that she had to squint.

"Elizabeth?"

Straightening in stunned surprise, she called, "John?" Relief and gratitude and love swamped her, making her almost giddy.

With a quick tap of his heels, he guided the horse nearer. He seemed almost wide-eyed, uncertain, something she'd never seen in him—and she felt the same way.

"Did you get lost from Wyndham's party?" he asked as he came nearer.

She shook her head, happiness fading into apprehension. What if he still wished to end their marriage? She would just have to convince him otherwise.

"Did Wyndham—did he change his mind?" he asked.

Again she shook her head.

"Then I don't under—"

"John, just stop speaking and listen to me." She slid down off the horse and approached him. When she stood below him, she rested her hand on his knee, surprised that she wasn't trembling. "I made a terrible mistake."

He sighed. "The annulment—"

"No, not that!" She gripped his knee in desperation, reminding herself that she could make this work. "I made a terrible mistake in leaving you."

His eyes went wide, and with the dawning of a smile, he lifted his leg up over the horse and jumped down in front of her. "Elizabeth? What are you saying?"

He gripped her upper arms, and she rested her hands on the front of his chest. She could feel his heart; how she ached to put her cheek there, to feel safe and loved. His hopeful smile was like the sun to her.

"I knew from almost the moment I left yesterday, that Lord Wyndham wasn't the man for me—he wasn't you." She reached her hand up and touched his stubbled cheek. "I love you, John."

When his smile died, a feeling of terrible regret swept through her. It was too late for them.

He squeezed his eyes shut, then took her hand in both of his and kissed her palm, cupping it to his mouth. "Elizabeth," he murmured hoarsely.

The low sound of his voice and the feel of his lips on her skin made her shudder.

Compromised

"Elizabeth, I made mistakes, too. I thought I was doing what was best for you by letting you go. But without you—I felt like half a man."

Tears filled her eyes as he kissed both her hands, then cupped her face.

"I love you, too," he whispered. "I was coming to fight for you, to prove to you that we could make this marriage work."

"And I was doing the same thing!" She stood on tiptoes and pressed her mouth to his. "Can it be true? Oh John, I promise I will never stop trying to make our marriage succeed. I will be such a good wife to you and never take you for granted. I want to love you and have your children and share everything."

He threw his head back and laughed, then swung her off the ground in a circle. "Elizabeth, I have so much to tell you. I'll never mislead you again, or keep secrets because I think I know better than you." He set her down and held her body close as he looked earnestly into her eyes. "But the most important thing is that I treated you unfairly, comparing you to another woman. That was no better than your parents' behavior, and I regret the heartache I caused you. I wouldn't blame you if you couldn't forgive me."

She felt giddy and free and wonderfully alive as she threw her arms around his neck and just held him, her cheek pressed to his, their hearts beating near each other's.

"Forgive you? Oh my love."

"But Elizabeth, why are you traveling alone?"

She looked up into his face. "When I told Lord Wyndham that I wanted to return to you, he was upset at the time and money he'd wasted, so he wouldn't help me. I

125

even promised to repay him for the loan of a gown—I would have included interest!"

John's eyes narrowed. "That fool left you to travel alone on these dangerous highways? Let us return, so that I may show his lordship the error of his ways with my sword."

"I don't care about him, John, only you and me. And if you give me one thing, then I can forgive you anything."

"Just tell me what you want."

"Our wedding night."

He went still, his smile fading, while intensity narrowed his brown eyes.

"Which is closer—the hunting lodge or the inn?" he asked swiftly.

She laughed and ran her hands down his chest, feeling the muscles she'd been longing to touch. "I don't need either. Do you?"

His mouth sagged open.

"I can't wait," she whispered, leaning up to kiss him.

With a groan, John crushed her against him and slanted his open mouth across hers. His tongue was an invasion she welcomed as his hands swept down her sides and hips.

"Elizabeth, are you certain?" he whispered against her mouth. "I don't want to force you—"

"Then I'll force you." She took his hand, and he gathered both horses' reins and followed her between the trees. She was nervous and excited and so very grateful that he loved her. Spending the rest of her life with him was all she could want.

"Wait, Elizabeth, I brought you something you'd left behind."

Compromised

He let go of her hand, and after a moment's fumbling with straps behind the saddle, he pulled out her crumpled, bent farthingale.

He held it out to her. "You wear anything you want, my love."

With a laugh, she took it and flung it into the trees, where it caught and hung from a branch like a flag of surrender. "I won't be needing that anymore." She grabbed his hand again and pulled him along behind her.

At the first small clearing in the forest, where the sun shown on a soft patch of moss, Elizabeth turned to face him. She unlaced the ties behind her neck, then pulled the gown down her shoulders and let it fall to the ground. She stood clothed in only her smock.

"Your turn," she said with a smile.

He was quick to pull off his belt and tunic, then untied his hose and codpiece, and pulled his shirt over his head. Her breath caught in wonder at how beautifully made he was, how broad and tall and proud. Only the loose linen braies hung low about his hips, barely hiding his enlarged penis.

His smile looked strained. "Your turn."

Wetting her dry lips, she reached for the hem of her smock and slowly lifted it over her head. The sun was hot where it touched her bare skin, and she thought she'd feel embarrassed. But John watched her like she was his every dream come true, which made her feel proud and humble and so thankful all at the same time.

"Your turn," she said, surprised to hear her own voice crack.

As the braies fell to the ground, she barely got to look before he crossed the small clearing in two strides and took her in his arms. The feel of his hot, moist skin and hard muscle pressed to every part of her sent a delicious rush of pleasure through her body. His lips covered hers, and she met his tongue gladly with her own as she explored his mouth. They were finally free to enjoy each other as husband and wife. She caressed his broad shoulders, his neck, his arms which held her so tightly. She kissed his cheeks and his chin and his ear, wherever she could reach.

"Elizabeth, you're bewitching," he murmured.

She bent to kiss his nipples, as he'd done to her. If anything, his shaft seemed to grow larger against her stomach, and she reached to touch it, amazed at the heat and hardness. It moved in her hand and she glanced up at his intent face.

"Does this hurt you?"

"God, no," he answered with a short laugh. "I'm just longing to be inside you."

She smiled. "Then why don't you?"

He groaned and closed his eyes. "Soon, my dearest."

He cupped her breasts in both hands and held the weight of them while Elizabeth gasped and swayed against him. "My goodness, that feels lovely," she breathed.

When his fingers teased her nipples, she gripped his arms, knowing her knees would buckle if she let go. As her head dropped back, he took her mouth in deep, languorous kisses, then spread kisses down her neck and behind her ear and across her shoulders. He dropped to his knees, and she held his head between her breasts for a moment, while the poignancy of her love for him almost overwhelmed her.

Compromised

But then his tongue licked along the curve of her breast and swirled about her nipple. She cried out, remembering now why she'd been unable to resist him that night in the garden. He worked magic with his mouth and his hands, until she was suffused in the passion he wove about her.

He suckled her, drawing her nipple deep into his mouth. Every tug was answered in the depths of her belly with a shudder of restlessness and yearning. He'd made her feel it before, and now finally she would understand the mystery of it.

Shaking and weak, she leaned into him, and he swept his hands down her hips and gripped her buttocks. His fingers met and teased the crease between them, and she moaned with the forbidden excitement of it.

She stood dazed in the middle of the forest as her husband trailed kisses down across her belly, and into the curls above her thighs.

"I want to taste every part of you, all over again," he murmured against her, spreading her legs wider so he could fit between them.

Elizabeth was excruciatingly aware that they were out in the open, beneath the sun, where anyone could see him doing this to her. But then she felt his tongue parting her, exploring her, and every thought in her head vanished except the desperate wish that he never stop. Every thrust of his tongue made her shudder with pleasure that was nigh unto pain. She held onto his shoulders, unable to look away from the sight of him between her thighs. He opened his eyes and they stared at one another until her legs gave way, and she was held up by his hands cupping her buttocks, pressing her against his mouth.

Then suddenly he dropped her back into the pile of her garments, spread her legs even wider and began to lick her with long, slow strokes that made her shudder and whimper and squirm. She raised her hips and gave herself up to this incredible mounting pleasure. When her legs were shaking, and she was rolling her head back and forth with little moans escaping her, he slid both hands up her body and rubbed her nipples.

With a hoarse cry, she plummeted deeply into the pleasure he gave her, shuddering and shaking as waves of it engulfed and swept her under. She lay still, gasping, as her awareness returned. Slowly she opened her eyes, and found him on his hands and knees above her, grinning.

She covered her hot face with her hands. He peeled her hands away, and when she opened her eyes she saw his concern.

"Are you all right?"

With a groan she threw her arms around his neck. "Compromise me again!"

"Oh, Elizabeth," he murmured, bracing his hands and settling his hips between her thighs. "This might hurt a little, but I promise you—"

"Please, just make me your wife!"

She felt the probing of his shaft against her swollen, sensitive flesh, and then he thrust home. The momentary pain she felt vanished as she watched him shudder and hold himself still.

"Is something wrong?" she asked cautiously.

John opened his eyes and came down on his elbows to kiss her. "There's nothing wrong with finding heaven, my love. It exists only in you, and I want to savor every moment."

Compromised

She touched him then, caressed him with all the love he inspired in her. He pulled out of her and entered again, and the joining of their flesh together renewed the wonder of her desire. He rocked against her, in and out, and she pressed kisses wherever she could reach his hot skin. She licked his nipples and was rewarded when he held still deep inside her body, trembling, his head thrown back, his face pained with concentration.

With a groan, he suddenly moved again, thrusting over and over inside her, until she knew by his hoarse cry that he had found the same release she had. She held his shuddering body against her, and knew a profound satisfaction. This was something she did well without even trying.

But the only person who made her feel this way was John, her husband, her love.

Exhausted and happier than he'd ever thought possible, John braced himself on his elbows and looked down at Elizabeth. He watched a gentle smile transform her, and knew he was looking into the face of true love. They would awake every morning in each other's arms, and the love in her eyes would be the last thing he saw each night before sleeping. Through fate or luck or a higher power, he had found the one woman who could make him feel whole.

Epilogue

Bathed in warm summer sunshine, Elizabeth rode her horse at John's side, no longer afraid of what lay before her. She knew he was impatient to introduce her to his family. He'd told her many details about his true home, his many estates. She was no longer angry at his deception, when memories of her own behavior in the first few days of their marriage left her wincing with shame. And the way he'd made it all up to her still left her blushing.

Coming to the crest of a hill and seeing the immense size of the sprawling castle before her made her catch her breath with the tiniest bit of apprehension.

John leaned from his horse and reached for her hand. "You can do this, Elizabeth. You can do anything."

"I tamed you, didn't I?" she answered, and he laughed.

When they rode down to the gatehouse now overflowing with people, she could tell by the love on John's face whom the members of his family were. His mother, brother, and his brother's wife rushed forward.

"Mother," John said, reaching across the distance between their horses to take Elizabeth's hand, "I went to London to court a fine woman and marry her, and I succeeded beyond any of my expectations. May I introduce Lady Elizabeth—"

"Malory," Elizabeth interrupted. "I'm Lady Malory now."

Compromised

John spoke with such pride in his voice that she was near tears.

His mother stepped forward as he helped Elizabeth dismount. The woman kissed her son, and looked between them wearing a happy smile upon her face.

"We received your missive days ago, John. We've prepared a great feast of celebration."

"That is so kind of you, my lady," Elizabeth said. She glanced at John's brother, so alike to him in height and coloring. "And you must be William. I have heard so many stories about you as we traveled north."

William took Elizabeth's hand and bowed over it. "Flattering ones, I hope."

William and John smiled at each other, as if they shared a secret joke. Elizabeth felt the same closeness to her brother Nicholas, and understood the affection and devotion between siblings.

Then William said, "May I present my wife, Martha?"

Elizabeth studied the woman that John so admired. Though some might not consider her a great beauty when compared to those at court, the gentle love shining in her eyes when she looked at her husband would make her the envy of every maiden.

Elizabeth curtsied to Martha, who blushed and glanced uncertainly at her husband.

"My lady, you mustn't," Martha said.

"But allow me to grant you the respect you deserve," Elizabeth insisted. "You and William showed my husband the kind of marriage he wanted. And he showed me. I would never have found such happiness otherwise."

"You are very kind, my lady."

"Please, call me Elizabeth. I want us to be friends."

The two women smiled at each other, and although Elizabeth felt hopeful for the future, a shadow crossed her mind at the thought of her first and dearest friend Katharine. On this last day of their journey, John had offered to return to London and help with the search. He had never taken lightly the absence of her friend, and now granted Elizabeth the most thoughtful, even romantic gesture. She hadn't believed she could love him any more but her feelings had grown even deeper after his generous, understanding words.

Her worry was interrupted by the arrival of several young children, the oldest carrying the youngest, not yet a year, who practically dove into Martha's hands.

William laughed. "And these are our children. Forgive their rudeness."

"I see no rudeness, just honest curiosity." Elizabeth smiled at the children.

John put his arm around her. "This is your new aunt."

One of the little girls winced. "You're very dirty."

"Joanna!" Martha exclaimed in a horrified voice. "Apologize at once."

But Elizabeth exchanged a smile with John. "She is only being honest."

"What has happened to the two of you?" Lady Malory asked, laughing and shaking her head as she studied the ruined garments they'd been wearing for days.

John put an arm around Elizabeth and hugged her to his side. "Our wedding trip, Mother. And what an adventure it was."

Elizabeth felt his love wash over her, protect her, and knew she'd come home.

134

Compromised

~The End~

Thank you for taking the time to read *Compromised*, the first book in the Secrets and Vows series. If you enjoyed it, please consider telling your friends or posting a short review where you purchased it. Word of mouth is an author's best friend and much appreciated.

Want to know when my next book is available? You can sign up for my e-mail newsletter at my website, www.GayleCallen.com.

After the excerpt, please continue on for "Behind the Scenes with Gayle," some extras I put together to enrich your experience of the book.

Next, turn the page and enjoy the first two chapters of *On Her Warrior's Secret Mission*, Book 2 of Secrets and Vows, where you'll discover exactly what happened to Elizabeth's best friend Katharine…

Thanks again!
Gayle Callen

Excerpt of ON HER WARRIOR'S SECRET MISSION

Secrets and Vows Book 2

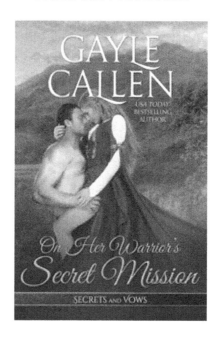

Chapter 1

Compromised

England
August, 1485

He stood with his back against the crumbling brick wall, fists clenched, his cowl falling against his perspiring cheeks. Once again, he heard the sound, a woman's low moan, quickly muffled. He took a deep breath and slowly leaned toward the corner of the wall, allowing himself to peer once and then pull back. In that moment, he saw the scene quite clearly under the eerie light of a full moon. A man, not one of the brethren, gripped a struggling woman.

Brother Reynold Welles hesitated in disbelief. When he looked again, a second man had joined them, wearing the black mantle of the Benedictine brotherhood and carrying a flickering candle. This man gestured, and they moved off toward the cloister court, the heart of the monastery.

What brother would need to have a woman brought to him? In the past, Reynold had known a monk or two who'd left one night, and come back with more satisfaction than they felt the peace of the church could give them. Though Reynold well understood the lure of women, he could not so easily break his vows. But bringing an unwilling woman to St. Anthony's Priory was sheer folly— or desperation.

The promises he had sworn to God and his family warred within him until his head ached. His sins still burned him, playing out over and over in endless nightmares. He should only care about his own redemption, not a stranger's. But he could picture the woman, bound and alone, forced here against her will.

137

How would he live with himself if she died, adding another death to his conscience?

~oOo~

Lady Katherine Berkeley yanked her good arm free and tugged at the filthy gag covering her mouth. For her trouble she received a quick blow to the head that set her ears ringing and almost knocked the blindfold askew.

A hot mouth pressed itself against her ear. "I don't want to hurt ye, liedy. They tol' me not to, but I will if ye make me."

The offending mouth remained a moment too long, and Katherine cringed. He had not hurt her so far, this brutal man who'd taken her as she rode through the woodland near her father's manor just two days before. But two days seemed like a lifetime of humiliation and terror. She had ridden blindfolded on a horse with more bones than flesh, perched on the thighs of a man twice her size. Gagged into silence, she had to repeatedly clutch the man's arm for a moment's privacy behind a bush. And even then, she could not know if he watched.

She shivered at the memory, as her silent captor dragged her forward. She was beyond exhaustion, beyond caring where she was. She only knew it was earth beneath her, not a galloping horse. They suddenly stopped, and her head bounced forward until her chin hit her chest. She heard a door open in front of her. A damp, sour smell assaulted her nose, and her eyes stung inside the wet blindfold.

"Here," an unfamiliar voice whispered.

"Ye're sure 'tis safe?"

"This place is falling into ruins. No one uses the undercroft for storage anymore. She'll keep safe enough long as she's gagged."

Compromised

As Katherine was prodded forward, she felt the ground squish beneath her leather slippers. The room seemed to stifle all noise except the skittering of tiny feet. A whimper escaped the gag. When she was released, she panicked, not caring that this was the same man who had so brutally abducted her. She clutched at his sleeves.

"Bind her!" the new voice said.

She frantically shook her head. Everything was dark and cold and foreign, except the man who had tried not to harm her. Yet now they yanked her arms behind her back, though she struggled. She wished she didn't know their secrets. Would they now kill her for her knowledge? She wished she was still safe at home, awaiting her betrothed. She'd promised to attend her friend Elizabeth's wedding; what had happened when she hadn't shown up? Surely they would send raise an alarm at her absence and contact her father. *Someone* would come looking for her.

Katherine realized she was alone when the door latched shut. Lurching to her feet, she waited a moment, listening. The air was still and oppressive with silence. She shuffled forward, then stopped, hearing the echoes far above her head. Where was she?

She edged sideways, trying to feel the door with her arm instead of her face. She banged her elbow and barely noticed the pain as she turned her back to run her bound hands over the door. Solid old wood, set firmly into a stone wall. She kicked once with her foot but made little sound. She did it again, harder. Did they intend to leave her here indefinitely, bound and gagged until she died?

Katherine tugged hard at the ropes biting into her wrists, hating her weak arm. She pulled and pulled until the blood trickled down her fingers. She staggered and fell, until the world retreated for a while and she drifted into an exhausted sleep.

~oOo~

Katherine came awake with a jerk, then winced at the shooting pain in her shoulders. Her hands seemed numb and unresponsive. She sat up and began to wiggle her fingers, then sighed as sharp little prickles tormented her skin from inside.

With her head bowed, Katherine forced herself to think through the last few weeks. She tried to tell herself she would have done something differently, but it wasn't true. She had learned of a plot against King Richard from a woman too terrified to publicly come forward. If Katherine did not escape soon, it would be too late. The king's enemies, whom he thought of as loyal friends, would turn on him. If only her chambermaid hadn't overheard her plans and told the kidnapper, betraying Katherine for a few coins.

But she couldn't give up as they all expected her to do. For the first time in her life she faced a true challenge, with no one to help her. Whoever was behind the plot to kidnap her obviously wanted her kept alive. Why? Was it because he had something more sinister in mind for her—or maybe because he didn't want her seriously hurt? She couldn't possibly know the person—could she? Dread quivered through her. She had to escape.

As quickly as her bound hands allowed, Katherine explored her prison, tripping over toppled barrels and ripped sacks of grain. By the time she returned to the first and only door, she knew she was in some sort of storage room, unused and containing no windows. She had tried to cut her ropes on a broken crate, and instead set her wrists to bleeding again. When the hours began to stretch out behind her, she felt the seedlings of true panic. Had her captor been decent enough on the journey, only to allow her to die forgotten? When the door finally opened, she felt a momentary relief that they'd remembered her.

When hands touched her she began to kick wildly. She prayed that the door was still open and she could escape. Arms gripped her, lifting her easily into an unfamiliar embrace as she struggled. This was a different man than her captor, harder, taller. In sheer terror Katherine fought him, until she felt fingers at her head, loosening her blindfold. She stilled immediately and waited to see what he had planned. A candle blinded her for a moment, then the man turned her to face him. She gasped in shock and fear.

A monk held her in a painful grip, a monk garbed in black with a cowl hiding his face. She shrank away as he lifted one hand, but he only motioned for quiet and reached for her gag. He peeled it off and her cracked lips stung unmercifully.

"My hands," she croaked.

He turned her around by the shoulders and she staggered at his strength. She suffered his rough touch until her hands were free, then whirled away from him. She rubbed her raw wrists and watched him suspiciously, waiting for his next move. After all, men who chose this life usually had some dark, hidden reason. But this one merely watched her, his head cocked to one side, a black hole for a face. Why didn't he remove the hood?

Katherine lifted her chin with what she hoped was a show of strength. "Are you releasing me?"

As he nodded, the cowl dropped forward and swayed.

She shivered with unease. "Then move aside and I will leave."

He pointed to himself, and then the door.

Katherine walked along the wall, never turning her back on the monk. "Nay, I will go alone. Is he gone yet?"

As his head dropped to one side, she almost leaned over to see his face, then thought better of it.

"The man who brought me here," she said.

He shrugged broad shoulders in answer.

"Do you not speak? Is your tongue damaged?"

He shook his head, then pointed to the door with more urgency, taking a step toward her.

Katherine shrank away from his menacing height and breadth, then crept around him, hoping he would leave her alone to escape. But she felt his breath on the back of her neck and shuddered as a chill swept up her spine.

The open door revealed a shadowy world of sagging stone walls and covered walkways, all lit by a cloudy moon. Across the courtyard stood an ancient church. The sound of deep voices chanting their prayers drifted on the breeze. A monastery. Who would think of looking for a noblewoman here?

She took a step forward and almost fell when a strong hand yanked her back behind the building. She fought the monk, terrorized by the thought of what those big hands might do to her. He merely shook her once like a child, then put a finger to his lips. He did have lips; she could see the faintest shadow of them. He pointed to himself, then her, then behind him, opposite the way she had meant to go. As she began to walk, she silently debated her childhood fears. She would follow this monk as long as he proved himself trustworthy. But only until she was free of the monastery.

From what Katherine could see by moonlight, everything around her was in a state of neglect. Walkways were pitted with holes where cobblestones used to be. Off to her right, dead branches hung from trees in the orchard.

She was so intent on not tripping, she only vaguely noticed that the chanting had stopped. But the monk in front of her went rigid, then put out a hand behind him to stop her. When his fingers almost grazed her chest, Katherine swallowed back the sour taste of nausea. Surely it had been an accident. He hadn't even looked back at her. But her hands started shaking. She held her weak arm with the other one, a habit she wished she could conquer. With her attention diverted from the ground, she began to stumble, falling farther behind him. The dark cowl swung back towards her and she almost ran in blind fear.

Katherine gasped when the monk veered toward the orchard at a sudden run. The practical side of her wanted to warn him that she didn't run well. She tended to twist ankles and bruise knees—not always her own.

When he motioned frantically, she took off at a fast run, hoping nothing lay in her path. Her skirts had a life of their own as they threatened to trip her or snag on overgrown plants. She pushed through the last weeds on the far side of the orchard, only to skitter to a sudden halt on the banks of a creek. She lost her balance and swayed forward, flapping her arms to stay upright. The monk caught her against him, his arm beneath her breasts, his head bent well above hers. Before Katherine could collect her fragmented thoughts, he pushed her forward along the bank. She walked as fast as she could, if only to escape the warmth of his breath from behind. She tried not to think of her parched throat. The cool water continued to lure her gaze but she would not get down on her knees before him to drink.

One of her slippers was captured by the mud. Katherine bent over to reach it, and the monk bumped into her backside. She almost shrieked, but instead gasped in outrage and straightened so suddenly that the top of her head slammed into his cowled face. He grunted.

"Be quiet—they'll hear you!" she hissed. "I lost my slipper!"

The monk raised his wool-covered head to the sky for a moment, then bent to search the mud. She grimaced when he handed the dripping shoe to her and motioned to her feet. Hopping on one foot, she put her useless slipper back on and continued alongside the creek. A wall loomed up out of the darkness. Her rescuer waded knee-deep into the water, and reached out to her.

"Is there a gate on the other side?" Katherine whispered.

He gestured for her hand once more.

"I can cross unassisted," she said, setting one foot into the water. She slid down a moss-covered rock and landed hard against the monk's side, her face striking his shoulder. Before she arched her head away, she smelled the clean scent of the wool and for a wild moment wondered what kind of monk he was. She came to her senses and pushed at the muscled wall of his chest, his obvious strength bringing back her fright. He turned her about like a doll until her backside was pressed into his hip and his arm encircled her chest. As her breasts were flattened in his embrace, and the water tugged at her skirts, Katherine began to feel faint. Her tongue was swollen and dry, and the water dripped its sweet temptation.

The monk's other arm snaked out before her, pointing downstream. She peered ahead, squinting.

"Does not the water go below ground?" she whispered.

She felt the slither of wool across her tangled hair as he shook his head. With his large hands at her waist he urged her forward, holding her up against the lure of slippery rocks and deep mud, until the monastery wall loomed above them in the shadows. Katherine braced both palms against the gritty stone.

"I can go no farther," she said softly. "Where is the gate?"

The monk dropped to his knees at her side, and pointed to where the water rushed beneath the lip of the wall.

Katherine swayed with disbelief but the monk held her up. "Under there?" she squeaked, watching in a daze as the water current caught his black robe at the waist.

He pulled and the flaccid muscles of her bad arm gave way beneath his strength until she fell to her knees on the bed of the creek. As the cold water chilled her, she gave in to temptation and scooped some into her mouth. He watched in silence, a darkly robed man in the shadowy moonlight of an ancient monastery. She ceased drinking and gaped at the black hole that was his face, repelled yet fascinated by what must lie beyond. He suddenly sank beneath the surface. She stared at the circular waves made by his departure until she felt a tug on her skirts.

"Oh no." She gasped a lungful of air and was pulled below.

Chapter 2

The water was so very cold. Katherine thrashed in the dark, frigid creek for a wild moment, sand swirling into her eyes. The current dragged her down river, and with her weak arm she could not swim effectively. Panicking, bursting with her need for air, she kicked herself upward and smacked her head on the thick stone wall of the monastery. She drifted motionless, dazed, forgetting to swim, forgetting everything. She was so tired.

Something yanked hard on her hair, pulling her forward. The last air bubbled out of her mouth as she broke the surface, gasping and gagging. Two strong arms lifted her out of the water. The monk held her like an orphaned kitten, dripping and bedraggled as she coughed weakly. Then he did the last thing she expected.

"Will you survive?" he asked politely.

Katherine gasped as she hung over his arm, her ribs compressed, her legs dangling. She managed to push wet strands of hair from her face and look over her shoulder.

"Did—did you say something?"

"I did," he said, in a voice deep and cultured, though muffled by his cowl. "I thought you had finally succeeded in killing yourself."

She kicked and squirmed until the monk released her. Pushing away from his chest, she strove to appear unaffected, to be brave, although the dark wilderness and this strange monk frightened her.

Compromised

"Kill myself?" Her voice lowered to a whisper. "You tried to drown me! Surely going over the wall would have been preferable."

"For me, perhaps. But I could not carry you, and you do not have the strength in your toes and fingers to climb. Now we must leave."

After picking up a dark bundle from the base of the wall, the monk moved to catch her arm. Katherine backed away.

"Leave? With you?"

The dark cowl remained still as he spoke from its depths. " 'Tis only a matter of time before we are discovered."

She felt almost as trapped as she had in the undercroft. She had no idea where she was, what she should do. The monastery walls rose behind her, stooped with menace. The monk stood between her and the forest.

"Where are we?"

"Western Yorkshire."

She sighed. She knew nothing of this part of England. But she did know that Nottingham—and the king—were farther south. But how to get there?

"We must leave," the monk repeated.

When he would have touched her, Katherine stepped aside and began to walk into the forest. The trees closed in around her, shutting out the last of the moonlight. She felt her way from tree trunk to tree trunk, scratching her hands on rough bark, tripping over roots. She refused to ask for help, although the monk continued to follow her silently.

Soon enough her knees grew weak with hunger and exhaustion. She was about to admit defeat, when the forest began to thin, and she could see glimpses of the moon between the branches. Stumbling to a halt at the edge of the woods, she looked out in dismay as the moon hung in the sky over a broad flat plain that sloped down away from her and seemed to stretch on forever.

"You are tired," his deep voice said behind her. "I know a place where you can sleep, where no one can find us."

He'd said "us." She shivered. But she was too exhausted to protest. She even allowed his arm to settle around her waist and steady her over the uneven ground. He led her to the left, skirting the edge of the tree line, until the sheer wall of a cliff rose up before her in the darkness. They walked beside the wall for less than an hour, both silent. An opening appeared in the cliff face, like a jagged crack straight down from the top of the moor. The monk disappeared into it, pulling her along behind.

Katherine staggered, disoriented. The earth seemed to press in all around her.

"We can rest here," he said. " 'Tis dry, protected from the wind."

He stood in the shadows. She couldn't see his eyes or his face to read his intentions.

She clasped her arm absently and turned away from him. "Why do you speak now and not before?"

"I observe the Greater Silence while within the monastery."

"The Greater Silence?"

"The brethren do not speak at night except to pray and sing."

She peered over her shoulder at him. He stood solid and dark as a mountain, blending into the night and the rock. She shivered as cold water dripped down her body beneath her ragged clothes. No sounds disturbed the peace. She was alone with him. She took another step away, wincing as her ankle turned on a stone.

"Why did you help me?" she asked.

There was a long moment of silence before he spoke. "You seemed in need of help."

His voice was suddenly deeper, and rumbled over buried emotions she could only guess at.

"How did you know I was there?"

"I saw them bring you into the monastery. I couldn't sleep."

Did Katherine imagine a hesitation? What wasn't this monk saying? Her doubts grew larger, heavier, until she felt overburdened by cares a young woman shouldn't have.

"I could not leave you to whatever they planned," he said softly. "I heard you crying."

His rough voice shook something deep within her. A new and dangerous sensation curled like heat through her stomach, and she convinced herself it was fear. "Thank you for your kindness. You can go back now."

He remained silent, still.

"Go on," she insisted. "I will be fine." She stared out from the crack in the cliff, squinting, looking for a road or path by moonlight.

"I cannot return," he said. "Your captor will know soon that I have aided you, and the prior might already have discovered my absence."

She felt the weight of guilt, which she immediately put aside. It was not her fault that this monk had helped her, risking his own position.

"Where will you go then?" she demanded.

149

There was no mistaking the long, tension-filled pause before he spoke, his words suddenly cold. "With you. You cannot possibly travel alone."

Katherine turned toward him, her skin cool and clammy with fright, as she swayed on the edge of defeat. She did not know this monk, nor did she want to. She'd never traveled farther south than York. And now she'd been dragged off to a ruinous monastery, bound, gagged, treated like an animal, rescued by a monk who'd almost drowned her. She wanted to laugh hysterically, and she wanted to weep at the same time. But most of all, in some deep hidden place in her heart, she wanted to prove to herself that she could accomplish one important deed before becoming wife to the Earl of Bolton.

But she was standing soaking wet inside a cliff at midnight, with no food, no horse, and no sense of direction. How would she ever get to the king?

"You cannot travel with me," she finally said. " 'Tis not—proper."

The monk set his sack down. "My lady, you are not thinking clearly. You must be hungry and cold. I have brought food and even a change of clothing. It would not do to look like a noblewoman."

She choked on a laugh and spread out her wet, dirty skirts. "How can you tell what I am?"

"Your voice, my lady."

She shivered. The moon overhead was about to slide behind clouds, leaving her in total darkness with a stranger twice her size.

Cold and wet and miserable, Katherine looked up at the monk. "Please, can you not just give me the food and leave me be? I don't want your help."

Compromised

"In all honor, I cannot leave a woman alone in the countryside."

"What do you know of honor?" she asked bitterly, remembering another monk so many years before.

The head of her rescuer tilted to one side, but he did not answer. Instead he lifted his hands to the cowl and began to pull it back. Katherine felt a deep thread of fear wind its way slowly up her throat, making it hard to breathe. She did not want to see his face, did not want to think of him as a man. He was a monk like the others, not to be trusted, having hidden reasons for everything he did. Yet she did not turn away as the hood fell in wet folds to his shoulders.

In the shadows of the night his face looked carved of rock, with a square jaw and a cleft beneath his thin lips. His brows hung heavily over the sockets of his eyes, turning them to blackness. When his lips turned up in the faintest semblance of a smile, she felt a strange chill.

"I cannot travel with you," she said. "Just give me the clothes and I'll leave."

"I come with the clothes," he said in a voice made more menacing by its softness.

"Then I will do without." She turned away and promptly tripped over her wet skirts, landing on her hands and knees in the dirt. As she fought tears, the monk picked her up under the arms as if she were a child's toy and set her on her feet.

"You need me," he said flatly. "Unless you can outrun me, I will follow."

"But why?"

He hesitated, and this time she could see anguish flicker across his face. Could she have imagined it?

"I cannot leave you to whatever dangers are out there," he said. "You are helpless against the elements, helpless against these men should they choose to pursue you. I still do not understand why they kidnapped a noblewoman, when for a few pennies, a peasant girl would have—" His voice broke off.

"Would have what?" Katherine demanded. Her face flushed with heat. "You think they took me for—themselves?"

"Perhaps a ransom?" he said quickly.

Refusing to answer, she shivered and remembered the two humiliating days at the hands of her captor. Again, it nagged at her, how careful her kidnapper had been not to harm her. The monk was right—they would try again. She knew their treasonous secret. And now that she'd escaped once, would they be so anxious to keep her unharmed?

"Why do you distrust me?" he asked, his head above hers, his voice deep and harsh. "What have I done short of rescuing you from an unknown fate at the hands of men who kidnapped you? I have offered my help at the loss of everything I have strived for at St. Anthony's."

"I can't trust you!" she cried. "I know you not. Yet you help me."

She covered her eyes with one hand. It hurt to remember that other monk, that "religious saint" her mother had trusted. No one had protected Katherine from him. If a man like that could claim a calling from God, anyone could. The next priest who cast a spell over her mother was little better, though he left Katherine alone.

152

Compromised

She was alone now, with no choice but to turn her life over to a man whose calling she despised, one who professed a need to help her but could give no true reason. She was too far away from King Richard's Nottingham castle, with no idea how to get there. The bleakness of her situation settled about her soul like a shroud.

"I shall spread a blanket for you while you change out of those wet clothes," the monk said, his voice only a sound in the darkness, but not unkind.

She hugged her arms over her chest, feeling the warm dampness of her gown. Change?

"The moon has left us, my lady."

"After I've slept," she said, wondering if she would fall over in sheer exhaustion. What did it matter if she changed now or in the morning?

Rough cloth was placed into her hands out of the blackness.

"You must change tonight, before you catch a sickness. This is an undergarment to protect your skin from the woolen gown. You can sleep in it tonight. Please obey me in this. I don't wish to watch you die."

"There's no privacy," she whispered, hugging the smock to her.

"I cannot see you."

She heard compassion roughen his voice, and her resolve to be strong crumbled beneath the onslaught. A tear slipped down her cheek as she loosened the laces at her back. She shrugged the bodice forward and pulled off the wet, tight sleeves. With her embroidered girdle gone for many days, the gown fell from her hips into a pile at her feet. If only her own smock were not soaked, she could sleep in it. Instead she peeled it from her body and stood there naked in front of a strange man, a monk, who she only hoped could not see her.

A sob caught in her throat. The linen scratched her skin as she pulled it over her head and down her body.

"Here is a blanket," he whispered, bumping her hand with his and finally grasping it. "Come down, lady."

As if she could be called "lady" after undressing in front of a monk and sleeping beside him wearing naught but a smock. She lay against the scratchy wool of the blanket, only vaguely feeling the weight of another blanket laid atop her. She told herself she was too tired to care that he lay close beside her. All that mattered was sleep, a sleep with no dreams. Yet the rise and fall of his chest stirred the blanket, and his even breathing kept time with the rhythm of her heart. He gave off heat that kept her as warm as any fire. She wondered if sleep would come.

~oOo~

Brother Reynold Welles came awake with a start, then remained still, listening. The slit of sky above his head was pale gray, heralding the coming dawn, illuminating the rough, gritstone chasm where they slept. For a brief moment, he wondered if it had all been a bad dream, but when he looked, she was there, stretched out on her back with her face turned toward him in sleep.

He inhaled sharply, smelling once again the scent of woman. He closed his eyes and tried to suppress the groan of sheer pleasure that threatened to escape. He could not remember the last time he had seen a woman, let alone been close enough to smell one. Sensations he had struggled for months to suppress now rose in chorus to distract him. He remembered a serving girl at his parents' castle, the white flesh of her thighs, the scent that lingered on her breasts. She hadn't been afraid of him, like so many others. He had buried himself in her, and the heat and warmth of her even now seemed so real. Just when he was resigned to the life of a monk, to serving God for his sins, this woman appeared, in need of rescue.

Reynold propped himself up on one arm and looked at her. He regretted it almost instantly, as the serving girl disappeared from his mind and a new woman took her place. She glowed with a quiet beauty, this dirt-streaked girl, with her honey-blonde curls draped over half of her face. Without thinking, he allowed his trembling fingers to touch her hair, to lift it away from her mouth. His hand looked so large and brutish beside the delicate bones of her face that he snatched it back as if burned. He told himself he was a monk now, that there was no turning back. A sly second voice whispered that he was only a novice, that his final vows had not been spoken.

But that was the path to the sins he had once committed. He had to help this woman because honor demanded it, because a good Christian brother always helped those less fortunate. Yet his gaze did not look for her soul. He saw long, golden-brown lashes resting on cheeks blushed red from the sun. Her face was heart-shaped, with lips soft and full for kisses.

Reynold broke into a sweat, but still he could not stop looking at her, could not move away even if the prior himself had come upon them. She was all soft and round and feminine, so small to his bulky body with its awkward height.

He suddenly saw the way his mind was moving. Lust was unforgivable—only her safety mattered. For just one moment, her white, still face reminded him sharply of Edmund's face.

My God, Edmund. It was still almost too painful to think of his brother, who had labored so long over books that his skin rarely saw the sun. That was what had brought Reynold to Katherine, her weakness, her need. He had tried to crush these things in his brother, as if such people weren't worthy of the great knight, Sir Reynold Welles. He had paid for that pathetic arrogance, paid over and over with his brother's blood. He had vowed to take his brother's place as best he could, to atone for his sins, to help any poor soul who needed him, no matter the task. And yet—

And yet he was a man who appreciated spirit and courage, of which he suspected this girl had aplenty. He would help her, though resisting her appeal might prove harder than any penance he had suffered.

Stretching out one arm, he rested his head upon it and continued to gaze at her. Her eyes suddenly opened and looked straight into his.

Look for the paperback of ON HER WARRIOR'S SECRET MISSION on Amazon, or the e-book at your favorite bookstore.

Books by Gayle Callen

The Daring Girls of Guernsey: a Novel of World War II

Secrets and Vows Series
Compromised
On Her Warrior's Secret Mission
The Knight Who Loved Me
The Bodyguard Who Came in from the Cold

The Brides Trilogy
Almost a Bride
Never a Bride
Suddenly a Bride

Highland Weddings Trilogy
The Wrong Bride
The Groom Wore Plaid
Love with a Scottish Outlaw

Brides of Redemption Trilogy
Return of the Viscount
Surrender to the Earl
Redemption of the Duke

The Scandalous Lady Trilogy
In Pursuit of a Scandalous Lady
A Most Scandalous Engagement
Every Scandalous Secret

Gayle Callen

Sons of Scandal Trilogy
Never Trust a Scoundrel
Never Dare a Duke
Never Marry a Stranger

Sisters of Willow Pond Trilogy
The Lord Next Door
The Duke in Disguise
The Viscount in her Bedroom

Spies and Lovers Trilogy
No Ordinary Groom
The Beauty and the Spy
A Woman's Innocence

Behind the Scenes with Gayle

Hello, readers! You can't be a historical romance writer without enjoying research. I was lucky enough to visit England several times. Since I took so many photos, I'd like to share them with you so you have a better idea of the scenes in my book. For more photos, check out the other books in the series.

Above is the St. Albans pub "Ye Olde Fighting Cocks," one of the oldest in England. The original structure is from the middle ages, and at times it was also an inn, so I thought you could imagine Elizabeth and John stopping here on their journey to Yorkshire. My husband says it was his favorite pub—and beer—on our trip. Inside, it's all dark wood and timbered ceilings, and you can really imagine what it was like hundreds of years ago.

On my most recent trip, I travelled with my youngest daughter, who was doing a semester abroad in London. We rented a car and drove from London to Yorkshire (on the left side of the road!), stopping at many places along the way. I could have made her visit castle after palace after manor, but I'm a kind mother, so we stopped to hike occasionally. This is Dovedale in the Peak District. We walked along the river (quite swollen in this photo) and eventually circled up around the hill in the back, where we got way too close to sheep for us city girls. You can picture Elizabeth and John travelling here, stopping to camp nearby and using this river for drinking and bathing.

Gayle Callen

Why I Love the Middle Ages

I have always been fascinated by the middle ages. In my youth I read many books on King Arthur, and was drawn to Mary Stewart's very different version of Merlin in her Arthurian saga that began with *The Crystal Cave*. But it wasn't until I started reading historical romance, specifically Kathleen E. Woodiwiss's *The Wolf and the Dove*, that I was hooked on the English medieval era.

I do a lot of research to make my books historically accurate, and often it inspires story ideas. I set the "Secrets and Vows" series in the 1480s after I first heard about the mystery of the lost Princes in the Tower. King Richard III was only supposed to be the Protector and guardian for his young twelve-year-old nephew, the new King Edward V. But the king and his nine-year-old brother disappeared in the Tower of London. Their bodies were never found, so Richard became king. There were many theories about who killed them or if they escaped; pretenders to the throne appeared for decades claiming to be one of them and the rightful king of England. If Richard had killed his nephew, he only reaped the rewards for two years before being defeated by Henry VII in the final battle of the Wars of the Roses. I found all the research fascinating!

When I heard that several of Richard's trusted noblemen secretly betrayed him, the idea for On Her Warrior's Secret Mission, the second book in the "Secrets and Vows" series, was born. My heroine Katharine overhears these traitors plotting. When she tries to warn King Richard, she's kidnapped and imprisoned in a broken

Compromised

down monastery where Reynold, a novice monk not yet ordained, has to rescue her.

Make sure you read all the books in the "Secrets and Vows" series. Here's a list of the books and how the characters are related:

Compromised
(Elizabeth and John)

On Her Warrior's Secret Mission
(Elizabeth's friend Katherine and Reynold)

The Knight Who Loved Me
(Reynold's brother James and Isabel)

The Bodyguard Who Came in from the Cold
(Reynold's and James's sister Margery and Gareth)

About the Author

After a detour through fitness instructing and computer programming, Gayle Callen found the life she'd always dreamed of as a writer. This *USA Today* bestselling author has written more than thirty historical romances and has won the Holt Medallion, the Laurel Wreath Award, the Booksellers' Best Award, the National Readers' Choice Award, and has been a nominee for RT Book Reviews Reviewers' Choice Award. Her books have been translated into eleven different languages.

The mother of three grown children, an avid crafter, singer, and outdoor enthusiast, Gayle lives in Central New York with her husband, Jim the Romance Hero. She also writes contemporary romances as Emma Cane.

Visit Gayle's website: GayleCallen.com

Made in United States
North Haven, CT
19 May 2022

19346171R00095